KU-662-506

"I'd say you've inherited your share of charm."

Would she have said that yesterday? Before he bought her lunch, before she met his family, before she heard what he had to say about his ex-fiancée?

Dario smiled. A slow smile that spread to his intense blue eyes. Isabel's heart thudded. If he touched her, her skin would sizzle. That was how hot she was.

The sound of the Puccini aria rose and filled the air. She didn't know what the words meant, but she understood pure passion when she heard it and when she felt it. Isabel's heart raced. The longing in the song matched the longing in her heart. A longing to hold and be held. To kiss and be kissed. That was all.

He was going to kiss her this time. She knew it.

Dear Reader

Can you tell that I love Sicily, with its mysterious inland mountains, its trendy cities, its rumbling volcano and its wonderful beach resorts? If you have any doubt, you'll be convinced of my love affair with this island when you read THE SICILIAN'S BRIDE. I've tried to capture a newcomer's fascination with the scenery and the people by giving an American woman a Sicilian vineyard, which she inherits from an uncle she never knew. Then I've put an obstacle in her path to achieving her dream of finally finding a home of her own. That obstacle is a wealthy and hard-working winemaker who thinks he deserves to have her vineyard—not her.

When my family and I vacationed in Sicily a few years ago I said to myself, 'I must set a book here.' Thanks to Mills & Boon for giving me the chance to share my passion for the delicious and spicy pasta dishes eaten in charming coastside restaurants, for visits to cathedrals and *palazzos*, and best of all for the people of Sicily—warm-hearted, opinionated, and incredibly generous to foreigners like me.

Best wishes

Carol

THE SICILIAN'S BRIDE

BY
CAROL GRACE

MILLS & BOON®
Pure reading pleasure™

All the characters in this book have no existence outside the imagination of the author, and have no relation whatsoever to anyone bearing the same name or names. They are not even distantly inspired by any individual known or unknown to the author, and all the incidents are pure invention.

All Rights Reserved including the right of reproduction in whole or in part in any form. This edition is published by arrangement with Harlequin Enterprises II BV/S.à.r.l. The text of this publication or any part thereof may not be reproduced or transmitted in any form or by any means, electronic or mechanical, including photocopying, recording, storage in an information retrieval system, or otherwise, without the written permission of the publisher.

® and TM are trademarks owned and used by the trademark owner and/or its licensee. Trademarks marked with ® are registered with the United Kingdom Patent Office and/or the Office for Harmonisation in the Internal Market and in other countries.

First published in Great Britain 2009
Harlequin Mills & Boon Limited,
Eton House, 18-24 Paradise Road, Richmond, Surrey TW9 1SR

© Carol Culver 2009

ISBN: 978 0 263 20779 8

KENT LIBRARIES AND ARCHIVES	
C153515954	
HJ	17-Nov-2009
AF ROM	£12.99

Carol Grace has always been interested in travel and living abroad. She spent her junior year in college at the Sorbonne, and later toured the world on the hospital ship *HOPE*. She and her husband have lived and worked in Iran and Algeria. Carol says writing is another way of making her life exciting. Her office is her mountain-top home overlooking the Pacific Ocean, which she shares with her inventor husband. Her daughter is a lawyer and her son is an actor/writer. She's written thirty books for Silhouette, and she also writes single titles. She's thrilled to be writing for Mills & Boon® Romance. Check out her website—carolgracebooks.com—to find out more about Carol's books. Come and blog with her fun-loving fellow authors at fogcitydivas.com

CHAPTER ONE

ISABEL MORRISON was lost. She'd been driving around on dirt roads for hours looking for the Monte Verde Vineyards. There were no signs at all out here in the country. The small rented Fiat was not equipped with GPS or air conditioning and she was sweltering in the September heat. She'd known it would be hot in Sicily, but not this hot.

No wonder there was no one around to ask directions. Only mad dogs and Englishmen were out in the noonday sun. And one American looking for her piece of the American dream, far far from home. All she wanted, all she'd ever wanted, was a home of her own.

The home she was looking for, if she ever found it, would be a place to start over. A place to put down roots at last. A place where no one knew what mistakes she'd made in the past. A place to earn a living growing grapes in a vineyard she'd inherited from an uncle she'd never known.

As an orphan, she'd been left on the doorstep of the home for foundlings with nothing but a basket and a blanket and a note asking the good sisters to take care of her. Which they had done, as best they could. She'd known nothing of an uncle. Least of all what he was doing in Sicily and why he'd left her a vineyard. All that mattered was that someone cared enough to leave her an inheritance—and what an inheritance! A home of her own. Not only that, but vineyards too.

She'd done everything she could before she'd left home: read a dozen guide books, taken Italian lessons and a short course in viticulture. She believed in being prepared and self-reliant. Being naive and too trusting had gotten her heart broken. Never again.

Now if only she could find the old villa—the Azienda— and the supposedly neglected vineyards on the Monte Verde Estate, she'd be in business. The business of settling in, growing grapes and producing the great little dessert wine, Amarado, that the place had once been known for.

According to the map the solicitor, Signore Delfino, had given her it should be right...over…there.

"I can have someone take you out there next week," he'd said.

"Thank you, but I can't wait until next week," she'd answered. Next week? She'd been waiting all her life for a place she could call her own and now she couldn't wait another day. She'd wondered if he was stalling. He'd tried to talk her into selling the place before she'd even seen it.

"I must advise you," he'd said, "the property is in some dis-repair from neglect. If you want my advice…" He cleared his throat. "You should sell it to a local family who are prepared to make you a generous offer. I can handle the details for you." The way he'd said it indicated she'd be crazy to turn the offer down.

"Please tell the family I appreciate their interest, but the property is not for sale." No matter how much they offered, she wouldn't sell, and she'd find it on her own, thank you very much.

On one side of the road was a rushing stream lined with eucalyptus trees, and on the other side, golden wheat fields lay next to vines heavy with fruit. The air was heavy with the spicy smell of the trees and the scent of wheat drying in the sun. But she couldn't figure out how to get to where she wanted to go.

Yes, it was hot and the air was dry. Yes, she was lost. But she was also nervous and scared at the prospect of actually turning grapes into wine that was good enough to sell in the upscale market. One thing at a time, she told herself. Maybe there would be a kindly old caretaker who would take her under his wing and show her how it's done. He'd say, *Your uncle talked about leaving the place to you. How you'd carry on the family tradition...Let me help you get started.*

She smiled to herself, picturing the scene. One way she'd dealt with rejection in the past was to lose herself in an imaginary world, to the dismay of her teachers and foster parents who accused her of being a dreamer. It was her way of escaping the hard edges of reality.

As a graduate of the School of Hard Knocks, she'd learned early on in life to have an escape route when life's problems got too overwhelming. Another coping mechanism that had come in handy to was to act in a confident and self-assured manner, especially when feeling the opposite.

Just when she thought she'd have to turn around and go back to the little town of Villarmosa and get more directions, she spotted a man picking grapes. Exactly the kind of man she would need to hire to work in her fields. Even if there was a kindly mentor on the premises, she'd still need laborers. The man in sight was strong, tall and muscular and obviously used to hard work. Being a local, surely he'd know where her vineyard was.

She was so excited she slammed on the brakes, and skidded to an abrupt halt.

He looked up. She grabbed the map, got out of the car and

walked toward the field where he stood staring at her as if he'd never seen a stranger here before. Which made her feel better about staring at him. She stared at his blunt nose that looked like it might have been broken a few times. She stared into his eyes, impossibly blue in a sun-tanned face.

Then her gaze moved down. He was shirtless, and his jeans rode low on his hips. Very sensible in this kind of weather. And very sexy too. She swallowed hard and tried to tear her eyes away from his broad chest covered with a light dusting of dark hair, but couldn't. Perspiration broke out on her forehead. She couldn't seem to take a deep breath. Maybe *this* was her property. Maybe he worked for her already and she'd be making wine this fall with his help. No, she couldn't get that lucky.

"Hello," she called when she finally caught her breath. *"Ciao, signore. Per favore, dove e la Villa Monte Verde."* A whole sentence. Maybe the grammar wasn't perfect, maybe her accent shouted out that she was a tourist, but she was proud of herself for trying. When she had tried to talk to the lawyer in Italian yesterday, he'd switched to English.

Not a chance with this rugged type. She wondered if all the hired hands were this gorgeous. It didn't matter. One reason she'd jumped at the chance to move to Sicily was for a fresh start and to avoid relationships, no matter how attractive the men were. In a new environment, with a brick wall around her heart and a system of warning bells in place, she was ready to take on a new challenge. She was willing to make mistakes along the way, just as long as they weren't the same mistakes she'd made in the past.

The man frowned and gave her a long scrutinizing look that made her pulse quicken and her heart race. From what she'd seen in the airport, Italian women were so chic, so effortlessly stylish, she must look positively shabby to him in her wrinkled shirt and the plain wash-and-wear skirt she'd pulled out of her suitcase. If he even noticed.

His gaze moved to her rental car across the road. She was close enough, just across an old wooden fence, to see a hostile look appear in those incredible blue eyes. She'd imagined people would be friendly here. Maybe she was wrong.

He didn't say a word. Hadn't he understood her Italian? Or did the place go by another name? "La Azienda Agricola Spendora?" she said hopefully.

"You must be the American who arrived yesterday," he said in almost perfect English. His deep voice with a slightly seductive accent sent shivers up her spine. A simple laborer he was not.

She let out a breath she didn't even know she was holding. "How did you guess?" she said lightly. "I suppose my Italian needs some more practice."

He shrugged as if he really didn't care if she was an alien from another universe or if she spoke grammatically perfect Italian. "What can I do for you, miss?" The words were polite, but his tone was cool, with a sardonic edge.

Never mind. She didn't have to make friends with everyone she met. For all she knew he was overworked and underpaid despite his ease in speaking English, and probably tired and thirsty. It was still possible she could hire him, even if he had a chip on his shoulder. She could use someone who spoke English and was a hard worker.

"My name is Isabel Morrison and I'm looking for my vineyard, the Azienda Spendora." She couldn't help the note of pride that crept into her voice. The words *my vineyard* had such a nice ring to them.

"I'll give you a ride. You'll never find it on your own," he said. He reached for a shirt hanging from the branch of a tree and put it on before she could protest. How many times had it been drummed into her not to take rides from strangers? This was the kind of stranger who set off flashing detour lights in front of her. Too well-spoken, too sure of himself, too eager to take her heaven knew where.

"Really, it's okay, I can find it. I've got a map," she said, hating the hint of nervousness in her voice.

"Are you afraid of me?" he asked, looming over her with all his six-feet-something and broad shoulders, shirt half-unbuttoned, blue eyes challenging her either to admit or forget her fears.

"No," she said a little too quickly. While a voice inside her murmured, *Well, maybe just a little.*

"I'm Dario Montessori and I live nearby. In fact, these are my vines." He waved an arm in the direction of the fields behind him. "I know everyone for miles around and everyone knows me. Come along. You might meet some neighbors."

"Now?"

"Why not? *Nussun tempo gradisce il presente,* as we say in Italian. Wait here. I'll bring my car and pick you up."

This was an order there was no resisting. Besides, she did want to meet her new neighbors. It would be silly to pass up an opportunity like this. After all, she wanted to fit into the local village life. What better way than to be taken around by a native? So she waited there until he pulled up in a red-and-black convertible with leather seats. No ordinary farmhand could touch this car with under a hundred thousand. Who was he really? Why was he going out of his way for her?

"If you're planning to kidnap me," she said with a touch of bravado, "Don't bother, because I don't have any rich relatives you could hit up for the ransom."

He slanted a glance in her direction. The look on his face

told her she'd just spouted the most absurd thing he'd ever
heard. "I've lived here all my life and I don't believe there's
been a kidnapping around here in one hundred years. Relax,
you're in Sicily now. As for the Azienda, I'm warning you,
when you see it and the condition it's in, I am certain you'll
be willing to sell it to me."

"It's funny," she said thoughtfully, "you're the second person
I've heard of who wants to buy it from me. Just yesterday…"

"That was also me," he said, turning up a bumpy, dirt road.
"Your solicitor was representing my family."

"The family that owns most of the land around here? The
family that makes prize-winning Marsala and exports
Cabernet all over the world?"

He nodded.

"Then you already know I'm not going to sell it."

"You haven't seen it," he said flatly.

"I saw a picture of it on-line. It looks charming."

"Hah," he said and shook his head at her ignorance.

So he too was trying to discourage her. In the photograph
the house appeared to be small, and it was located on rugged
terrain at a fourteen-hundred-foot elevation. But it looked
snug and was situated in a picturesque grove of olive trees and
grape vines.

"That picture was taken some years ago when our family
owned it. Antonio let it fall apart."

Isabel bristled at the criticism of her uncle, although he
might have deserved it. As a family member she was surely
entitled to criticize him for allowing the place to disintegrate,
but this man was not. At least not in front of her. "Perhaps he
had reason," she suggested.

Dario gave her a steely look that told her more than words
that there was no good reason.

"Did you know him well?" she asked.

"He kept to himself. But it's a small town. Everyone knows everyone."

"I see," she said. But she didn't see. What was her uncle doing in Italy?

"He left the place in a mess," Dario said.

"I'll clean it up," she insisted. "I don't mind hard work. I know how to paint and make repairs. I've done it before." She'd even done it in her San Francisco rental unit when her landlord had refused to pitch in. Here she'd have the incentive of improving her own property.

He raised his eyebrows, probably surprised by her determination. He hadn't seen anything yet. She'd been criticized for years for being strong-willed after she left the orphanage.

"Isabel's a very headstrong girl," the social-service workers had agreed. She'd been moved from house to house, from foster family to foster family. No wonder no one wanted her with her bright-red hair and her stubborn disposition. No wonder she was passed over for younger, sweeter, more obedient little children. No one wanted to adopt a child with "inflexible" or "rigid" written on her reports.

It hurt to be overlooked, standing there, tall and gawky, enduring being examined and finally rejected time after time. But she got over it. Even when she was officially declared unadoptable because of her age, it had just made her more eager to grow up and set out on her own. This was her chance. She'd show them.

"Do you know anything about growing grapes?" he asked.

"Some, but I know I need to learn more," she admitted.

"Do you know how to prime a pump, irrigate fields, fight off frost? Do you know how hard it is to fertilize volcanic soil, are you prepared to wait for years to harvest your grapes?"

he demanded. He was almost enjoying this inquisition, she realized. She could tell by the way he looked at her, the way he raised his voice to be sure she caught every word.

What really annoyed her was the way he assumed she was far over her head and had no business even trying to break into *his* field.

"Or are you in love with the *idea* of growing grapes," he continued, "and of bottling your own wine?"

She bounced out of her seat as they hit a dip in the road. "Years?" she said. "I can't wait years. I need to make wine and make a living from it. Surely it's possible. I'll hire help. If it's so hard to produce wine on the property, why do you want to buy it?"

"It is hard, even for us. But we have experience. Historically, it's our land. Has been for centuries. For hundreds of years most Sicilian wine was shipped off the island, to be blended into other wines. But now we're getting the attention from the world markets we deserve. Twenty-six generations of Montessoris grew grapes there before we were forced to sell it to your uncle a few years ago."

"Forced?"

"It's a long story and it doesn't concern you. We had a sales slump, followed by financial problems which induced us to give it up, but we've recovered and now we want the land back where it belongs. To us. What difference does it make to you? You've never seen it, you've never lived on it or farmed it. You didn't have picnics there, eat the grapes off the vines or swim in the pond. It means nothing to you."

A pond? She had a pond? She'd stock it with fish, swim in it and watch the birds drink from it. Now she was sure she'd never give it up. She sat up straight in the leather bucket seat. "You're wrong. It means a lot to me. A chance for me to do something different, to earn a living from the land my uncle left me."

"Your uncle never grew a single grape there."

"That doesn't mean I can't. I haven't seen the property, but it's mine and I plan to live there and make it my home. It's my right to settle there, my chance to make a fresh start. Surely everyone deserves that."

He shook his head as if she was naive and stupid. She'd been called worse. "I don't know what you've been doing," he said, "but if you want a fresh start, why don't you buy a hotel, start a newspaper or open a café? All of those would be easier for a newcomer than making wine. Take my word for it. Viticulture takes time and patience and a feeling for the land."

"I appreciate your advice," she said with all the manners she could muster in the face of his blatant cynicism. "But you have to believe me when I say I'm prepared to do whatever it takes to succeed."

He continued to steamroll over her plans for the future as if she hadn't spoken. "Want some more advice?"

Before she could politely say no, he went on. "Get a job. It's an easier way to make a living than making wine. Make some-place else your home. You know I could be taking you to a totally different property and you wouldn't know the difference."

Startled, she asked, "Are you?"

He turned to look at her as if she'd accused him of cold-blooded murder. Wordlessly he pointed to a crooked hand-carved wooden sign on the side of the road, and said "Azienda Spendora."

She let out a sigh of relief. He wasn't kidnapping her. He wasn't trying to fool her by taking her to another property. She was here. This was all hers. It was a dream come true. Or a nightmare. As soon as they pulled up in front of the house she saw what he meant.

There were tiles missing from the roof and cracks in the stained cement walls. She got out of the car and stifled a wave of disappointment. Whatever she felt, she couldn't let him see her frustration at the house's failings. He'd interpret it as a sign of weakness and just renew his futile efforts to buy it from her.

"You don't have to stay," she said. "I'll just look around and catch a ride back."

"Catch a ride?" he asked incredulously. "This is a private road. No one's been on it for months, not since your uncle died."

"Was there a funeral?"

"Of course. What do you take us for, savages? The whole town was there."

The implication was that she was the only one missing. Obviously he thought she had no sense of family obligation. Maybe he thought *she* was a savage.

"I didn't know he existed until I got a letter from the lawyer." She took a deep breath. "Don't worry about me. I'll walk back."

He skimmed her body with a cool, disdainful assessing gaze as if wondering whether to believe she hadn't known her uncle. He took in her short skirt, her white shirt and the strappy sandals she'd thought perfect for a hot Sicilian summer day, but which were hardly sturdy enough to walk miles down that rutted dirt road. Okay, so she was dressed all wrong. She wasn't Italian and she was out of her element. Why couldn't he give her a break, cut her some slack?

"I'll stick around," he said. "It won't take you long to realize this is not the place for you."

The man was maddening with his dark pessimism. She wished he'd leave. She'd rather walk barefoot over hot coals than know he was waiting for her to cave in and give up her inheritance.

She turned to look at him. Puzzled, she said, "Stick around? Where did you learn English?"

"From a tutor," he said in his incredibly sexily accented English. "Being in the wine business, my father had all six of us learn English, the universal language of trade. Bernard taught us all the slang and swear words he knew. They've been quite useful."

"I can imagine," she murmured, surprised that he'd deigned to favor her with such a long response. How long would it take her to learn Italian with all the slang and the swear words she'd need to live here? The difference between his privileged background with tutors and a large family and the way she'd been brought up was mind-boggling. She wondered if he knew how lucky he was. He probably took his family for granted. Most people did.

Instead of waiting, he followed her onto the veranda, stepping carefully over rotten boards and through the front door that swung open and creaked on rusty hinges. When a giant spider-web brushed against her face, she stifled a scream and lurched back so fast she bumped into him. He put his large hands on her shoulders to steady her or more likely to keep her at a distance, and she fought off the temptation to let him prop her up for a moment while she caught her breath. But Isabel Morrison would never rely on anyone but herself again. Not even for a moment. Instead she straightened her shoulders and forged ahead.

"It was just a spider," she said, more to herself than to him. If she didn't talk to him, maybe he'd go away. Or at least wait outside and let her explore on her own. With his imposing build, the brooding expression in his blue eyes, his way of speaking English that gave a new meaning to everything he said, he was impossible to ignore. She couldn't concentrate on the house. Not when he filled the place with his tall, masculine presence and his overwhelming confidence. All she knew was that no matter what its flaws, no matter how much he offered her for it, this house was hers and she was holding on to it.

Behind the house was the small pond dotted with water lilies. She leaned down and dangled her arm in the cool water.

"For irrigation," he said.

"Or swimming," she said. She pictured lawn furniture, a striped awning, and herself cooling off in the fresh water on a hot summer day in her very own pond.

He braced his arm against the stone wall and surveyed the scene. Was he resentful of her enjoying her own pond? Or was he simply remembering summer days when he had swum with his siblings here and feeling sorry that he never would again? From the look on his face she doubted he had any happy memories at all. What was his problem? Was it really only her and her ownership of this place?

His dark hair was brushed back from his face making his strong features stand out like those on a stone carving. He might have first looked like a farmhand, but now she could see him for what he was, the aristocratic lord of the manor, totally accustomed to having his way. To acquiring whatever land he wanted. And full of resentment at knowing this land was hers now.

"I'd avoid the pond," he said curtly, "unless you're not afraid of water snakes."

She pulled her arm out of the water and dried her hands on her skirt. Spiders, snakes, what else?

"You can see it hasn't been used for years," he said. "Your uncle…"

"I know. He neglected it. I know why you sold it, but why did he buy it from you?"

"Probably thought he'd cash in and make a fortune from the grapes. A lot of people have the idea it's easy and profitable to grow grapes and make wine." He pointedly looked right at her, leaving no doubt about who he meant. "It's an illusion. Outsiders often can't tell the difference between a burgundy and our local grecanicoa, let alone how or when to harvest an Amarado grape. It's hard work."

"I don't doubt it, but…"

"I know, you don't mind hard work. Believe me, you have plenty of it ahead of you."

She wanted to say he had no idea of how much this place meant to her no matter what condition it was in. She also wanted to ask him how and when to harvest these special dessert-wine grapes, but that would just confirm his suspicions that she was no different from her uncle, both ignorant dreamers. Maybe she was worse, since she hadn't even paid for the place. She didn't even know what she was getting.

"The first spring frost he let the vines freeze and came roaring down the mountain to take refuge in the valley and never went back." He shook his head with disgust.

"He was out of his element. What did you expect?"

"I expected him to sell it back to us before he died. But he was just as stubborn as you. All I want is the land back," he said. "Back in the hands of someone who appreciates the *terroir*, the soil, the land where these grapes are grown. Is that so hard to understand?"

She straightened and put her hands on her hips. "Give me a little credit. I didn't just take the next plane over here. I did my homework. I am prepared to appreciate the *terroir* as much as anyone. Even you. And I haven't insulted *your* relatives, you know, as you have my uncle."

"Go ahead. If you met them, you'd see my younger brother

is immature. My mother is domineering. My grandmother hopelessly old-fashioned. My grandfather is stubborn and opinionated but hard-working. Years ago he planted some of these vines, nurtured them, picked the grapes and bottled them. I take responsibility for their loss. Now I owe him and the whole family to get them back."

She didn't understand why he took responsibility or why he owed them when it was a family operation, but she couldn't mistake the hard edge to his voice. He was not only determined, but he had his whole family to back him up. She was outnumbered. It didn't matter. She had the deed to the land. They didn't. Sure she felt bad for his grandfather, but for once she was going to put herself first.

They couldn't force her to sell—unless she couldn't sell her wine because it wasn't good enough or because what he said about waiting years to see any profit was true. Or unless something else unexpected happened. Even in the heat of the midday sun, a cold chill ran up and down her arms. Had she made a huge mistake by coming here? Thinking back, all the surprises in her life had been unhappy ones except for this inheritance, which she took as a sign her luck had finally changed.

She noticed Dario hadn't mentioned a wife in his list of relatives. Which didn't mean he didn't have one. Anyone who looked like him was bound to have a woman in his life. But who would put up with that bitterness she heard in his voice or that single-purpose determination that left no room for anything else? Were those the same traits he saw in her? Surely she wasn't bitter, although she was certainly determined. He shouldn't begrudge her a small piece of land if he owned half the valley.

She'd like to meet his family, just because they were her neighbors and she wanted to fit into the local society, but they probably already hated her as he did for refusing to sell her land to them. Nonetheless, she envied him. What wouldn't she give for a big family she could tease and criticize and love despite their failings?

"What does your family think of you?" she asked. Maybe she was the only one who saw him as a difficult person to deal with. She doubted it. Not with that iron jaw, ice-cold blue eyes and stubborn chin. Or did he suddenly turn into a devoted grandson and lovable sibling when he was home? That was hard to imagine.

"Cold, ruthless and heartless. They say I'm different because I'm not relaxed and easygoing like a true Sicilian. I'm too determined, too driven, even obsessed. When things go wrong I don't shrug and say tomorrow will be better. I *make* it better. That's why…" He stopped in mid sentence, with his gaze fixed on her, as if he could make her see she had no chance against a formidable foe like him. She could imagine what he was going to say…*that's why I will take possession of this land and you won't.*

"But they love you anyway," she suggested. She hoped she didn't sound as skeptical as she felt.

He didn't answer. After a moment she filled in the silence. "You're very lucky. I never knew my parents. I never knew any family at all. No grandparents, no home, no family. I was an orphan." She kept her voice light, as if being an orphan was no more important than being brown-eyed or left-handed. She hated being on the receiving end of pity. But how she'd envied the kids with a home and a family, especially those with grandmothers. The kind who baked in kitchens that smelled like fresh bread, wore aprons and had laps to curl up in. How did she even know they existed? From picture books and from other kids. Certainly not from experience.

"I grew up in foster care," she explained.

He looked puzzled but he didn't say anything. She began to feel foolish for going on about her background when who cared, really? Maybe it was that he had no idea what she was talking about.

"Never mind, it's not important. You say my uncle never made any wine while he was here?"

"He wasn't here that long. Breezed into town from America or God knows where, bought the vineyard, walked away from the vineyard and soon afterward he died. No one knew much about him. Where he really came from, why he was here at all. Some people said he was on the run from the law in California. Who knows? It was clear he had no idea what it took to run a demanding operation like this. All those wasted grapes. Whatever wine there is was made by my family and it would be in the cellar."

Dario led the way to the kitchen where stone steps led to the wine cellar. In the kitchen they passed an ancient cooktop tilted to one side. The place reeked of cold and loneliness. It would be a job making it livable, but she could do it. There was an old wooden icebox and an oven with its door hanging open. It wasn't quite her dream kitchen, but it could be.

It was as if someone had been in a big hurry to get out of here. If Dario hadn't been right on her heels, Isabel might have allowed herself a moment of respect for the man who'd left her this place, but with Dario around, she pretended she wasn't affected by the depressing sight.

"Needs a little cleaning up," she said matter-of-factly. After all, no house was exactly the way you wanted it. There were always improvements to be made.

"It needs more than that," he said. "You haven't got running water or electricity or heat."

"I don't need heat, not in this climate."

"You will. If you stay."

"I will stay," she assured him.

As if he'd orchestrated it, a huge rat ran out from under the sink. She screamed, slammed the ice box door shut and jumped up onto an old wobbly wooden kitchen chair.

He shook his head, as if the skittish behavior of women was no surprise to him at all. To him she was just another woman over her head and unable to cope with hardship. Was it so strange she was frightened of rats? It didn't mean she was a defective person.

After a pause he said, "I thought you wanted to see the cellar." He held out a hand to help her off the chair. He might despise her and dismiss her as unfit to live here, but she had to admit he had manners.

Isabel took a deep breath. "Of course." No rat would keep her from her goal. No single-minded Italian would either, no matter how gorgeous he was, how blue his eyes were or how irresistible his accent was. He had no idea how many people had told her she was crazy to quit her job and go to Italy. Everyone she knew advised her to sell the place sight unseen, buy a house in California with the money and keep her job.

That was the sensible thing to do, but for once in her life Isabel didn't do the sensible thing. She needed to make a move. Get away from everyone who knew what a fool she'd been. A big move that would force her to be more self-reliant, to face new challenges with a new strength of purpose. To turn her back on her past and friends who treated her with concern and the sympathy she didn't want. She'd come five thousand miles and nothing would keep her from doing what she'd set out to do. And finally, she'd never give her heart away again, not when it was finally healed and whole.

This man had no idea how humiliating it would be to give up, to go home and admit she'd made another mistake. If she had a home, which she didn't. It would take more than a rat in the kitchen, more than a hole in the roof, more than a hostile neighbor. Much more.

She took his hand and gingerly got down off the chair, then walked with all the dignity she could summon down the stairs to the damp, cool basement. Again he was right behind her, his warm breath on her neck, though she would have preferred to explore alone, to find some hidden treasure like an old bottle of some fabulous vintage on her own.

The walls were lined with racks and racks of wine in dusty bottles. Some were empty, their corks lying on the floor, but others looked well-aged but possibly still good. How would she know? He pulled a bottle off the wall and held it up so she could see it from the light that filtered through the small dusty windows. "Nineteen ninety-two," he said. "My grandfather's Bianco Soave. Sealed with wax. That was a good year, a gold-medal year." He pointed to the seal affixed to the label.

"I guess some years are not so good?"

"With grapes as well as life," he said, as a cloud passed across his handsome features. "Some years are best forgotten." He wasn't looking at her. For all she knew he was talking to himself. Even in the dank semi-dark cellar she could tell from his expression he wasn't just being philosophical. He meant something had happened to him, and whatever it was, he had not forgotten it. She wanted to ask him how someone like him, surrounded by a big supportive family and acres of productive grapes would have even one bad year? How bad could it be? Bad enough to sell the place to her uncle, but it couldn't have been as bad as last year was for her.

"Was it a drought or a fungus?" She'd read either could devastate a vineyard.

"Yes," he said, but he didn't elaborate.

She could understand if they'd had losses due to a disaster out of his control. But maybe it was something more personal. If it was, she'd never find out any more. Not from him.

She could understand his not wanting to talk about it. Last year had been a nightmare for her, the worst of her life, and she'd done her best to hide her shame and embarrassment from the world.

Then she'd got the letter from the lawyer and her life had turned around. Coming to Sicily to claim her inheritance was the easiest decision she'd ever made. This would be her good year. She would make it happen. And one of these days she too would win a prize for her wine. Her lips curved in a half smile as she pictured the gold labels on the bottles, labels she would design herself.

She sent a sideways glance in his direction. His hand was wrapped around the wine bottle and he was watching her as if he knew she was dreaming a dream that wouldn't come true. But it would. As if he was waiting for her to give up. Give up? On her first day? He didn't know her.

After a long pause he broke the silence. "Not discouraged?"

She shook her head. "Of course not. The wine is yours," she said waving her arm at the racks that lined the stone walls. "All of it. Take the bottles with you."

"Legally it's yours," he said coolly. "But I'm curious to see how this one has held up."

He scraped away the wax with a knife hanging on the wall and popped the cork with a rusty opener, then he tilted his head back and held the bottle to his mouth. Fascinated, she watched the muscles in his throat move while he drank it. Her mouth was dry. He handed the bottle to her. His fingers brushed her hand and goose bumps broke out on her bare arms. It was the cool damp basement that made her shiver, not this tall, dark Sicilian stranger.

"Try it," he ordered. "Tell me what you think of it." She knew what he thought. She could have no educated opinion. So why did he even ask?

She put her lips where his had been and tasted the wine and him at the same time. She felt a quiver of excitement. Maybe it was second-hand contact with his lips, maybe it was the old fermented wine. It wasn't fair to put her on the spot this way, testing her to see if she knew anything about wine.

Unnerved by the way he stood there, arms crossed, way too close in that small space, his eyes glittering in the dim light and brimming over with self-confidence, she couldn't think of a single original thing to say.

"*Ciao,*" came a voice from somewhere above them. "*Chiunque nel paese?*"

"My brother," he muttered. Then he swore in Italian. At least it sounded like swearing.

So much for the bonds of Italian brotherhood, she thought as he brushed by her on his way up the stairs.

CHAPTER TWO

DARIO took the stone steps two at a time leaving the American heiress behind. That's all he needed—his brother interfering just when he was finally making progress. At least he thought he was. It was hard to tell when she kept insisting she wasn't discouraged. But no woman in her right mind would take on a run-down operation like this. Most women he knew wanted a beautiful house, land, money, excitement and more.

Naturally the woman he compared all others to was his ex-fiancée, Magdalena, who'd made it clear the life he'd offered her was not enough. Surely this woman would have to agree, sooner rather than later, that this run-down dump of a place was not enough for her, no matter what the long-term possibilities were, and run back to where she came from, which was where she belonged.

"What are you doing here?" he asked Cosmo, who was standing in the stone patio, his car parked in front of the house.

"I heard from Delfino the American woman might be on the property. I wanted to say hello and welcome her on behalf of the family."

"Are you out of your mind?" Dario demanded, struck by his younger brother's immaturity and lack of common sense. "Welcome the woman who has already refused to sell the property back to us? The woman who's keeping Nonno from realizing his dream before he dies?"

"Nonno's dream or yours?" Cosmo asked.

Dario ignored the question. He knew what his brother thought. He knew what the whole family thought of him. They thought he was obsessed with trying to recover this land they'd written off long ago. Maybe he was. But maybe he should be. Because it was his fault they'd had to sell the land, and now it was his responsibility to get it back. It was so obvious. Why couldn't they understand that?

"What were you going to do, bring her flowers and roll out the red carpet?" Dario asked.

"Of course not, but be honest, Dario, you're the one who cares more than anyone about getting the place back. Give it up."

It was true. No one in his family had any idea how important it was for him. How much he blamed himself for what had happened—and would continue to blame himself until he'd got the property back and their wine won the gold medal. Then and only then could he put the past where it belonged. Until then...

"It's gone," Cosmo said. "Get over it. Stop blaming yourself."

"Easy for you to say," Dario said. "It's my fault we had to sell. You know it's true."

"Forget it," Cosmo said. "It's over. We have vineyards enough. Let this one go. I came by to see for myself if the new owner is as beautiful as I heard," Cosmo said.

Dario shook his head. "You heard wrong. How do those rumors get started? She's not beautiful at all." It was true. Her mouth was too large, her nose too small. Her hair was the color of copper in the sunlight, but that was definitely her best feature.

"So she's not beautiful. What is she like?"

"Just offhand, I'd say she's stubborn, proud, determined

and naive. And overconfident. No idea what it takes to make wine. As soon as she realizes this place isn't for her, she'll be on her way. But right now she's wavering." Unfortunately that was just wishful thinking. He didn't detect any sign of wavering in this woman. "If you don't leave now you might say the wrong thing and she'll be here forever. It's not fair to her to encourage her."

"Encourage her?" Cosmos teetered on the edge of indecision. "I just want to meet her and say hello."

"Not today."

His brother wasn't happy about it, but after a few more exchanges, he finally left and Dario breathed a sigh of relief. It didn't matter what the new owner looked like, she was new, she was a challenge, and he didn't trust his brother to stand up to her. He'd feel sorry for her when he heard she was an orphan and forget the goal, which was to convince her to sell by pointing out the obvious: this was not a place for a novice, a woman on her own, a foreigner who knew nothing about viticulture. It was in her own interests either to find another house in Sicily or go back where she came from. He only wanted what was best for her—and for his family of course.

Though feeling sorry for an heiress didn't make sense, his little brother was a flirt and a playboy and loved to have a good time. In other words, a typical Sicilian. He was easily swayed by a new girl in town with a fresh face as well as a few curves in the right places. He had charm and affection, yes, but those were traits not needed today.

Dario knew from painful experience what his brother ignored or wouldn't believe. That women are masters of deceit. They were seldom what they seemed. Beautiful or not, they could look innocent and act vulnerable, but they were hard as polished marble and equally strong-willed, self-centered and capable of lies and deception.

When Isabel emerged from the kitchen, a bottle of wine under her arm and a smudge of dirt on her cheek, Dario knew his brother would have stood there, mouth open, gaping at the American heiress, taken in by her apparent lack of pretense and that dazzling red hair and pale skin. No, she wasn't beautiful, but she was striking in a way Dario had never seen before. She had a certain freshness and large helping of pride of ownership in her new acquisition—the Azienda.

Good thing his brother had left. He could just see Cosmo falling all over her, offering Italian lessons, sightseeing and God knew what else. Just what he himself might have done before he'd met Magdalena. And had his eyes opened and a knife stuck in his back.

The American was the new girl in town, with something undeniably seductive about her mouth and her body. Dario would have to be blind not to notice her long shapely legs. She had soft brown eyes that widened in surprise, and a rare smile that tugged at the corners of her full lips. Yes, his brother would have been smitten at first sight and would have rolled out the red carpet for the intruder.

Dario knew better than to be swayed by a pretty face framed with hair the color of autumn leaves, no matter how innocent she seemed. He'd been burned once. Never again. Even after more than a year had passed, his mistake in trusting Magdalena rankled like the sting of a wasp.

His approach, the correct one, was to keep his distance from the heiress, show her the worst of her property and then pounce with a generous offer. It would be kinder in the long run than sitting by and watching her struggle but ultimately fail.

"My brother just stopped by."

"I'm sorry I didn't have a chance to meet him," she said. "Why didn't he stay?"

"Another appointment," Dario said. "Maybe some other time."

"I found another bottle of wine I'd like to try." Isabel held up two glasses. "Would you like some?"

She was offering him his own wine? He clamped his jaw tight to keep from erupting in pent-up frustration. Yes, it belonged to her now, but still. He wanted to pound the wall to relieve his irritation at watching her play the hostess role. Even with the smudge on her cheek and dirt on the sleeve of her shirt, she looked like the lady of the manor. It was a heady feeling he could tell by the look on her face, and if this scenario played itself out, she'd never want to leave, however difficult the job of making the place livable. He had to put plan B into operation as soon as possible.

"I don't know wine the way you do, but I think it's aged well, don't you?" she asked him after they'd both tasted it.

"Not bad," he said and set his glass down on a ledge. "We won a bronze medal for this if I remember right."

"You must have won many medals."

"We have, but some contests are more important than others. The Gran Concorso Siciliano del Vini is coming up in a few weeks. We plan to take away a gold this year."

He didn't want to brag or look overconfident. But this was going to be their year. Winning the medal and getting the Azienda back. Two victories that would erase the losses of the past once and for all. He knew it. He felt it. If he kept a hawk eye on the land, the vines and the wine production, they'd end up with the prize and the best dessert wine Sicily could produce too.

He was proud of their wine, proud of the medals they'd

won. Nothing wrong with letting her know that. He turned to Isabel. "Now that you've seen the place, it's time to go."

"I haven't been upstairs yet."

What could he say? You won't like it? Knowing her, that would guarantee she'd insist she would like it. She didn't yet know about the bedroom off the kitchen where the servants once lived, and he sure wasn't going to tell her. Instead he led the way up the narrow staircase, Isabel following behind him. There it was, a small room with a narrow sagging mattress on a metal frame. And better yet, a huge gaping hole in the ceiling.

"It needs major roof repair," he said. As if she hadn't noticed. No one in their right mind could say anything positive about a hole in the roof. But she did.

"Why?" she said. "If it doesn't rain, it will be wonderful to look up at the stars at night."

He groaned silently. There was no point in telling her bats would fly into the room. She'd probably welcome them. He'd never met anyone like her. There wasn't a woman in Sicily who'd accept living under these conditions. What was it about this woman? Was she really capable or just stubborn and unrealistic?

"I know it needs work," she said, a trace of defiance in her voice. "I know there's no running water or electricity, but, as I said, I'm not afraid to pitch in and get things done. And I'd like to hire someone to help me."

"That won't be easy," Dario commented. It was true. All the able-bodied men were at work in the vineyards. "Most people are busy with the crush."

"Which reminds me, I want to see the vineyard."

"Of course." That, Dario thought, could help matters; she'd see how withered the vines were.

They went back downstairs and out into the hot sunshine

where they walked up and down the path between the old vines. Dario followed behind Isabel, noticing the way her hips swayed enticingly as she walked, how the perspiration dampened the back of her neck, admiring in spite of himself her red-gold hair, which she'd tied back, gleaming in the sunlight. But only as he would admire a painting by Titian, with cool detachment. His detachment was cool until his mind jumped to the thought of her as the half-clothed subject of a lush Titian painting.

A surprising jolt of desire hit him in his chest. He'd been immune to the allure of women since his affair with Magdalena had ended so disastrously. Could his libido be alive and well again? Maybe all it took was knowing he'd finally recovered and was back in charge of his life and his vineyards. And then a glimpse of a Titian-haired heiress didn't hurt as long as she didn't stay too long. All he asked was for life to return to the way it was—pre-drought, pre-fungus, pre-Magdalena. He was almost there. He felt a new surge of energy, a feeling of hope close at hand, as close as the vines on either side of the path.

Dario deliberately turned his attention to picking and tasting a grape here and there, much safer than watching the woman. Another surprise—the level of sugar in the neglected fruit. Soon they could be turned into the superb dessert wine they were famous for. If. If the woman would only be reasonable. They should win the gold this year for either a red or a white. They would be back on top, and the world would be theirs again.

Finding that Magdalena was deceiving him was one thing, but losing his head over her so that he'd been negligent in running the vineyards was ten times worse. He blamed himself for the whole mess. He'd learned a valuable lesson. No matter how tempting, he would never fall for any woman again. His family didn't believe that. They thought his turning into a loner this past year was only a phase. He didn't think so.

This year if all went well, they could be on top again with a win at the Concorso for their Ceravasuolo. Let his family call him obsessive. He didn't care. It was better than being careless. He buried himself in his work. It was his choice and his obligation. Someone had to worry about the wine and family's land holdings. His father was busy in Palermo, his grandfather was sick. So that person was him. Let his sisters suggest he get out and find a girlfriend. It wasn't going to happen. Not now. Not ever.

Isabel paused to pick some grapes and licked her lips. Even as a beginner unaccustomed to tasting wine grapes off the vine, she was struck by how sweet they were. She felt a quiver of excitement. These were special grapes. She'd read about super-sweet grapes, old grapes that had been neglected. Her grapes.

She turned to Dario, whose blue eyes were narrowed in the bright sun. "These are delicious," she said. "Are they the same grapes that produce the famous Amarado dessert wine?"

He hesitated. Didn't he know or didn't he want to tell her? Finally he nodded.

She realized he didn't want her to know. He wanted her to get discouraged and leave. Sell out to him. He was sorry she'd stumbled on her own high-quality grapes. She could tell by the way his mouth was set in a straight uncompromising line, and by the creases in his forehead that this was the last thing he wanted her to know.

"I've tasted that wine. It's delicious. After I did some research on the Azienda Spendora I went out and found a few bottles of old Amarado in an upscale beverage store. It's very expensive in the States, if you can even find it," she said thoughtfully. "A high-end wine. It could be a huge moneymaker."

"I wouldn't count on it."

She slanted a glance in his direction. He knew. He must know how valuable it was. "No wonder you want this vineyard so much. It's because of the Amarado. I can't believe it. These are all mine and I'll make this superb dessert wine. I *can* make a go of it. I know I can. I can make money. Live off the land and show the naysayers."

She paused, struck by the look on his face. What had she said to make him glare at her like that? A muscle in his temple twitched. Was she excessively bragging? Or was he just upset because they were hers and not his grapes? "You didn't tell me about these grapes."

"You didn't ask me," he said shortly. "Don't get too excited," he cautioned. "It takes more than just picking and fermenting the grapes to make a decent Amarado."

"You don't think I can do it. You don't think I have what it takes."

"Do you?"

Suddenly a shaft of uncertainty hit her. What made her think she could compete in a wine market where her competitors had been doing this for decades? Maybe she was dreaming. Maybe she was overconfident. He was right. It wasn't going to be easy.

"Yes. I'll make it work," she insisted. "Why shouldn't I?" She was proud of how certain she sounded when inside a small voice asked who she thought she was. How did she think she could compete as an outsider?

"Why? Because you can't possibly pick your own grapes," Dario said. "You have acres of vines. It's backbreaking work and you have to know what you're doing. You don't want to do work like that. That's not women's work."

Women's work? She frowned and bit back a retort, something like *Even in Sicily, haven't you heard of equal rights, equal pay and equal opportunities?*

It seemed as if he hadn't heard a word she'd said. Hadn't she made it clear she'd stick it out and produce the wine these grapes were famous for even if she had to pick the grapes herself?

"You can ruin the whole crop by doing it yourself or hiring unskilled laborers. What you should do is take a vacation then go back where you belong." He took her arm and half pulled her back to the driveway where his car was parked.

"I *am* where I belong," she said, stepping out of his grasp before she got into the car. Her face was hot. Perspiration dripped from her temples.

Once they were in the car, he drove so fast her hair was whipped around her face in the wind. "This is my land," she reminded him. "I don't care how hard it is, I'm going to get those grapes picked and make my own wine from them if I have to do it myself. Which I can't believe I will have to do. I don't know what kind of women you're used to dealing with or what work you expect them to do. I'm not a fragile flower who'll sit at home knitting, waiting for some man to come along and take care of me. And I'm not a tourist. I'm here to work and I'm here to stay."

"Fine," he said after taking a moment to digest this. "Stay. But stay somewhere else. I'm prepared to make you a generous offer. You can take the money and buy a house with a garden. Something you can manage on your own."

"I'm not interested in another house. I'm staying here on *my* land and in *my* house. My uncle wanted me to have it, not you. The Azienda Spendora is not for sale."

"You haven't heard our offer."

"I don't need to."

"Look," he said as he stopped the car and turned his head to turn his penetrating gaze on her. "I'll make a deal with you. Let me take you around the countryside to look at property for sale. If you don't see anything you like, anything that compares with the Azienda, then I'll give up. I'll stop bothering you. *Dio*, I'll even help you find the workers you need."

"And if I don't agree to this fruitless trip around the countryside? Because I can tell you right now…"

"If you don't agree, and you don't come with an open mind, then I promise things won't be easy for you. You have no idea how hard it is to find workers, and you won't find many friends either."

Her face paled. She tried to turn her glare at him but she couldn't keep her lower lip from trembling. Oh, she put on a game face, but he'd finally made a dent in her self-assurance. He'd threatened her. He must be desperate for the land. But not as desperate as she was to hang on to it.

"All right," she said. "I'll go with you, but I'm warning you…"

He almost looked amused. As if she had some nerve warning him when he'd just threatened her. He held up one hand, palm forward. "No warnings, no conditions. I'll pick you up at eight tomorrow morning."

"Wait," she said. "I never met any neighbors. You said…"

"Tomorrow is another day," he said. But he didn't apologize or make any promises. She had a feeling he never did. Then she saw she had a flat tire.

The next morning Isabel had half a mind to cancel. If she'd known Dario's phone number she might have. She dressed carefully in Capri pants and a tank top, then changed into a sundress, but after surveying her image in the full-length mirror in her hotel room, she changed into blue jeans and a T-shirt then back to the Capris.

As if it mattered. The man had barely glanced at her yesterday, and when he did look her way he didn't see a living breathing person who only wanted what she deserved, or even a pesky, tired, jetlagged tourist, he saw an obstacle standing in his way.

Take yesterday, when he'd fixed her flat tire for her. At first he'd looked at her as if she'd done it on purpose to annoy him. Without a word, he took his shirt off and opened the trunk of her car to remove the spare tire and a jack. She tried not to stare at his bare chest, since the sight of those well-toned muscles made her knees weak, but she couldn't help it. Since her auto club didn't have service in Italy, she had no choice but to watch him repair her tire. She hoped he didn't think she'd repay him for his work by selling him her vineyard.

She watched closely while he propped the jack into the fittings on the side of the car. Squatting next to the car, his broad shoulders were covered with a sheen of sweat as he started cranking the jack. He muttered something that she didn't understand. Probably something like "Damned helpless American women."

She kneeled down next to him, her skirt pulled to one side, her bare knees pressed against the hot pavement. All in the interest of learning how to change a tire by herself some day. Kneeling there, she was all too aware of the essence of earthy macho male emanating from his half-naked body. Just being that near him made her feel as if her insides were melting. Or was that just the temperature outside?

He handed her four small metal objects he'd taken off something, his rough palm brushing her fingers. He smelled like ripe grapes and the hot Italian sun. She felt faint. No wonder. It was way past lunch time and she hadn't had anything to eat for hours, just half a glass of wine. Maybe that's why she felt so lightheaded.

When he'd replaced the flat tire with the new one, she said *"Grazie,"* and gave him a grateful smile.

He didn't smile back. Didn't praise her attempt at speaking Italian. She didn't expect him to. He'd used up all the good will he had for her, if any. He hadn't introduced her to a single neighbor. Hadn't even introduced her to his brother. But, after him changing her tire, she could hardly complain. He might be the lord of the manor and the owner of all the land around here, but he wasn't too proud to do a menial job and she admired that about him. Another man might have called a garage and hired a mechanic. If only she'd told him then to forget about showing her other properties. It wouldn't do any good, but he'd made up his mind. Well, so had she.

CHAPTER THREE

AFTER a cup of delicious cappuccino and some hot rolls on the sun-dappled veranda of the lovely Hotel Cairoli the next morning, Isabel told herself to relax. Let him show her around the countryside. He'd soon realize he had no chance at all of her changing her mind. She'd simply treat it as an opportunity to see something of the area in the company of an attractive Italian man who knew his way around. And maybe finally meet some locals. Never mind the gorgeous Italian found nothing remotely attractive about her, especially her personality. That was his problem, not hers.

By the time he arrived, she'd almost convinced herself she could treat him like her driver and nothing more. But then she saw the heads turn when his impressive car pulled up and he got out wearing khaki cargo pants and an expensive polo shirt that matched his eyes and did nothing to conceal the taut muscles in his arms.

Before she could get up and go to meet him, he'd walked through the place like he owned it and taken a seat at her table. The waitress was scurrying to bring him a cup of coffee and a plate of fresh hot rolls. She was beaming at him as if he was her long-lost brother, and it seemed everyone in the place knew who he was and lost no time in either shaking his hand or putting their arms around him as if they hadn't seen him for years.

It was obvious he was not only part of a big family, he was part of a community as well. She felt a pang of envy. How long would it take for her to feel this way? She couldn't wait for twenty-six generations to pass by.

"Are you enjoying your stay?" he asked, his blue gaze zeroing in on Isabel as if she was the only one on the veranda. His attention was flattering. Or it would be if she didn't think he had an ulterior motive. He'd either decided to change his tactics, or he'd decided to enjoy the day and forget his only too apparent motive. Knowing him it must be the former.

"Very much. But I'm planning to move out either today or tomorrow."

"Why, what's wrong?" he asked with a quizzical lift of his eyebrows.

"Nothing, the people are nice and the beds are very comfortable. But I didn't come here to loll about in a luxury hotel when I have a perfectly good house of my own." She felt her cheeks redden. They both knew it wasn't "perfectly good." She braced herself for his retort.

"Ah," he said. But that was all. No mention of the lack of water, heat or electricity. Which only made her worry about these things more. It was much easier to be brave when she had to convince him at the same time. Without a rival to fight with, she felt strangely deflated.

"As you know, it's harvest time and I need to be picking grapes." She waited for his predictable comment about how hard the work was and how busy all the real workers were, but it didn't come.

Instead he drained his cup and said, "Ready?" then stood and pulled her chair out from the table. She had the feeling the whole hotel staff was standing there watching as if he were a movie star on location as she got into his car and pulled away. She had to admit he was better-looking than any movie star she'd ever seen.

Did his attention to her raise her status in the community she longed to be part of? Either the group on the terrace at the hotel were shaking their heads, thinking she was a fool for going off with the Sicilian playboy who might even be married or they were cheering her on, thinking she'd be a fool for not running off to spend a day with the sexiest man around these parts.

It didn't matter, this was not a date. He was not interested in her nor was she in him. He was showing her around only because he thought he'd achieve his own goal that way. She was spending the day with him for the same reason, to get what she wanted. But she couldn't help being curious about him and his family.

She leaned back against the soft leather upholstery and let the sun shine on her face. She felt no need to make conversation since he seemed to be lost in thought, maybe pretending she wasn't there. He'd insisted on showing her property, he hadn't said he'd enjoy it. His eyes were hidden behind his wraparound sunglasses, one suntanned arm braced on the open window. His mind was somewhere else, no doubt.

To distract herself from looking at Dario, thinking about him and admiring his hands on the wheel, his bronzed arms and his skillful driving, she tried to identify the different kinds of trees they passed—oak, elm, ash and maybe beech. There might even be cork and maple. In the hills above them, farm animals grazed. It was a peaceful and bucolic scene, one most tourists never saw. She told herself to sit back and enjoy it while she could. Tomorrow and the next day and every day after that she'd be at work in the vineyard.

Glancing at his profile out of the corner of her eye, she thought he was just as gorgeous from that viewpoint as he was full-on, with his broken nose, his solid jaw and high cheekbones. From a strictly impersonal viewpoint of course. If he wasn't married, she wondered why not. Was it his surly personality, or was that side of him reserved for her benefit?

He pointed to a village perched high on a hill. And finally he spoke. "Casale," he said, "one of the first towns taken by the Normans from the Arabs who took it from the Saracens who took it from the Byzantines."

"So I'm not the first foreigner to claim land here."

"Not at all. But you should know Sicilians are tough people. We may seem to give in at first, but we're just rolling with the punches. We may occasionally be defeated, but it's just temporary. We've been around for centuries through good times and bad. Everyone wants something we've got—our land, our crops and our climate. For six thousand years the Greeks, the Romans, the Arabs, the French and the Spanish, they've all come and seen and conquered. They've all left their marks. But eventually they moved on. And we stayed on. We're here for good."

Isabel took her time taking this all in. Not just the history lesson, but his taking the trouble to instruct her. "Of course you are," she said at last. "You're Italian and you belong here."

"I'm Sicilian," he said firmly. "The Italians are just the latest colonizers who've come to strip away our wealth." She knew what he thought. Whether Italian or American, she was in the same category as the other intruders. Was that the real reason he was taking her on this tour? To make her aware of her place in history? Where were the villas he wanted her to see? The land for sale?

"There's a rather nice Roman villa over there that was

buried in the mud for seven hundred years until it was discovered in 1950. You should see it."

"Why?" she said. "Is it for sale?"

One corner of his mouth twitched as if he might possibly smile. That would be a first. He shook his head. "Don't worry. I haven't forgotten why we're here. I'm glad you haven't either." He turned down a side road. The villa was open to tourists, but today there were only a few.

"Villas were more than simply vacation homes for the wealthy Romans," Dario explained, "there are outbuildings which could house more family and servants and workshops as well. The owner and his family lived in this section with fifteen rooms, an underground central heating system and mosaic flooring."

"Like your house?" she asked. How rich was he? How big was his house?

"Mine? I live by myself in the gatekeeper's cottage on the family property. It's pretty simple. No mosaics, no grand facade like you see here, where even the stables and servants' quarters are faced with some kind of beautiful stone frontage. The Romans wanted to make a statement, let the world know they were rich and powerful. Our family…" He paused as if he might be about to divulge a family secret. "Our family isn't like that."

Oh, no? she wanted to ask. Then why did they need her property? Why couldn't they be happy being the biggest landowners for miles around? Why did they have to have her tiny little vineyard?

Lived by himself, he said. She wanted to ask what he'd told his family about her. Maybe nothing. Why had his brother taken off yesterday before she could meet him? Was Dario protecting her or his brother? Maybe she was so insignificant she didn't even warrant an introduction. Just buy her off, she thought they'd say. We don't want to see her. Let us know when the sale is done and we can celebrate.

She paused to admire a well-preserved wall mosaic that pictured dolphins flanking a vase and a central rosette with a knot motif.

"Even the Romans loved dolphins," she murmured.

"Why not? They're intelligent, acrobatic, and they seem to like us humans. If you leave by ferry, you'll see them in the waters off Messina."

She stiffened. "Why do you assume I'm going to leave? I'm not. I'm staying." What did she have to do to prove to him how determined she was to stay? And why?

"Shall we go?" he asked without answering her question. Maybe he sensed her frustration. Maybe he even enjoyed pushing her, watching her respond, hoping she'd tire of fighting back. But she wouldn't. Her heart was hardened and her will power intact. She'd had years of practice.

She didn't even waver when he drove to the coast where white sandy beaches contrasted with the clear blue sea. There above the beach was a small cottage for sale with a balcony overlooking a garden. Standing on the stone terrace she caught her breath at the stunning beauty of the view.

The scent of lilies and wild herbs filled the air. The contrast to her own run-down house was striking and he knew it. This was the kind of place you could move into and never have to worry about a hole in the roof. She imagined a garden full of tiny tomatoes bursting with flavor, a kitchen with sauce simmering on the stove. For a moment she felt her heart longing to have all that and more.

Once she had wanted love too, but no longer. It was folly to think of having a family and sharing her life with them.

She'd tried that and it hadn't worked. In the past, every time she thought she'd found a family, they'd sent her on her way. When she grew up and finally fell in love, she'd thought her life had turned around. Her mistake. One she would never make again. She was on her own again and always would be. Now more than ever.

"The best part is that it's only a few kilometers from our largest archeological site. It was built by the Greeks and has the best example of Doric columns you'll see anywhere. If you're interested in that kind of thing."

What could she say? She didn't care about history? She was indifferent to archeology? On the contrary. She'd love to visit the site and study the relics of the past, but she had to make a living. No, it was better to say nothing negative, just tell him she'd think about it.

"How much is it?" she asked.

"Don't worry about that," he said. "Let's just say it would be an even trade."

"But how would I earn a living?"

He didn't have an answer for that. She knew what he was thinking, that she wasn't likely to make a living from her grapes either. But she'd show him. She'd make wine and she'd sell it if it was the last thing she did.

Instead he looked at his watch, which appeared to be a Swiss collector's timepiece with multiple dials and a view of the precision movements through the face. How like him to have a watch that matched his car—expensive, luxurious and well-appointed. He obviously had never known what it was like to need money the way she did. Except for that glitch when they had to sell her uncle their vineyard. She still didn't understand how that had come about. When she'd asked if it was a drought or fungus he'd said yes. But what had actually happened?

"Time for lunch," he said, expertly masking his disappointment, if he had any, to her reaction to the beach house. "You look hungry." If he thought an expensive restaurant lunch would soften her up to sell to him, he was wrong. That didn't mean she wasn't hungry and intrigued when he drove a half hour to the city of Pallena and parked just outside the old Roman walls.

She reminded herself this was his idea. But no matter how many historic sites they'd visit or how many fine lunches he'd treat her to, she couldn't be bought.

"This is a favorite restaurant of mine," he said, leading the way through an old arch and down a flight of steps to a narrow pathway that led to the walled city. "I hope you like it."

Like it? How could she not? There was an entrance to the place through a door in the medieval wall, where they passed through the lounge area to the large bustling restaurant upstairs.

"It was once a Gothic palace," he said, pointing to the high stone walls and graceful arches above them. As it was almost two o'clock the place was full of Sicilians who were talking, eating, drinking, and lingering over tiny glasses of Limoncello or small cups of strong coffee.

The smells of roasting meats and slow-cooked sauces filled the air. Isabel hadn't realized how hungry she was until she sat down across from Dario at a small table in the corner and looked at the menu.

She had no idea what to order. Were they supposed to have all five courses or just a salad or perhaps some pasta? She was relieved when he ordered lunch and wine for both of them.

Dario was curious to see what Isabel thought of the wine he'd ordered. It was his personal favorite. If he knew her, she'd have something to say, whether he agreed with it or not.

When it came to the table, he took a sip and nodded his approval. Isabel noticed the Montessori label.

"Your own wine," she noted. "Doesn't it bother you to have to pay for it?"

"Not at all. I'm glad to see they serve it here. It's a '97 Benolvio that my grandfather was especially proud of."

She sipped it slowly. But did she appreciate the subtle nuances in the taste? How could she? "Very nice," she said. "Did it ever win any prizes?"

"No, but it should have. We may make a wine aficionado out of you yet."

Surprised, she blurted, "Was that a compliment?"

He only shrugged. Maybe she'd learn to appreciate wine, maybe not. That wasn't his purpose in bringing her here. He didn't know exactly why he'd done that. Maybe because it was a place few tourists knew about. Or maybe because this was where he and Magdalena had often come and he wanted to exorcise the demons. To prove to himself he could enjoy the food and the atmosphere without thinking about her.

While Isabel was looking around the room, he glanced at her. She wasn't the beauty Magdalena was. But he wasn't the only man looking at her. Maybe it was because she was American, maybe it was her hair, a spot of riotous color in this dim restaurant. Other heads turned and other eyes watched her as she drank her wine along with drinking in the ambience.

If only he could get her to relax she might put aside her defenses and realize what everyone knew—the Azienda was not the place for her. He gave her credit for wanting it and wanting to make a go of it. Nothing wrong with a healthy dose of ambition. But she wouldn't last a week in that place. Maybe not even a day and a night. No matter how much gumption she had, she'd have to be rescued from the bats who flew into her bedroom and the boars that tore up the vines at night. Who else would do it but him?

Maybe it was the wine or the light from the sconces on the palace walls, but from across the table he thought she looked more at ease. Her shoulders were no longer stiff as if on military alert, her cheeks had a healthy flush and her warm gaze scanned the room. Maybe she just needed some time to get used to the idea of giving up the Azienda. He could only hope.

His gaze was fastened on her, studying her, trying to figure her out. He was glad he'd brought her here. She ought to see something of Sicily besides a worn-out vineyard. She should leave here with happy memories of the island and not feel she'd failed. He knew what that felt like and he wouldn't wish it on anyone. She'd go home with a pocketful of cash, enough to do whatever she wanted to do. Or even stay here, buy a cottage, one that needed no remodeling.

He was encouraged to see her let down her guard. And not just because it would make his job easier. She usually looked like she was braced for the worst. What had happened in her life to teach her to be on alert all the time?

"What did you do before you left California?" he asked. He'd planned to make polite conversation. But he found he was curious about her.

She set her glass down. "I was a graphic artist."

He glanced at her hand on the table, noticing her graceful tapered fingers. He could imagine her in front of an easel with a paintbrush in those delicate fingers. "You're an artist?"

"Of a sort. It's not like being a painter or a sculptor. I create images for the purpose of selling products for customers."

"Don't you ever want to paint or draw something for yourself?"

"I'm not good enough."

"Why don't you draw pictures of grapes instead of growing them? I guarantee it will be easier."

"I was thinking I could do both. I plan to design a wine label for myself and my wine." She picked up the bottle from the ice bucket on the table and studied it. "Look at this. The label doesn't say anything about your wine. And it's dated as well. You need something that tells the customer about your product. Something fresh and new. This is old."

"So is the wine," he said.

"It would make a big difference in customer perception. I could design something new for you if you like."

"Thanks, but no thanks. This is the Montessori label. It's what people know. What they're used to. And what they look for when they want a fine wine. May I remind you you know nothing about our wine or our tradition?"

"Maybe not, but I know something about labels and what sells." She leaned across the table, her eyes glowing, an intensity in her gaze he hadn't seen before. She was all earnest and eager to share her knowledge with him. She had confidence in herself, he gave her that.

"How are your sales?" she asked.

"Fine," he said brusquely. He would never admit to her they could be better. Why risk changing a label and bucking tradition on the slim hope sales might be improved? A gold medal would improve their sales. Nothing else.

"Then keep your labels," she said, "but when I bottle my wine…"

He felt as though a cold wind had blown across the table all the way from the Alps. She'd said *when* not *if.* She was a dreamer, and dreamers are not easily convinced to do the right thing. The practical thing. If he didn't find her a house to buy today, he'd promised to help her harvest her grapes. He'd better think of something irresistible to show her.

She was cut off in mid sentence when the waiter brought

the appetizer he'd ordered, a small plate of gnocchi in gor-gonzola-and-pistachio sauce. Her eyes widened and she inhaled the aroma of the rich sauce. She took a bite and nodded slowly. At least she appreciated good food. Maybe even good wine too, though he doubted it. How could she when she hadn't been around it all her life?

After the waiter served them a salad of vine-ripened tomatoes garnished with fruity olive oil and fresh basil, Angelo, the owner came by to slap Dario on the back and tell him it had been a long time, and he'd missed him. Fortunately he didn't mention Magdalena. Even though he surely knew what everyone knew—his fiancée had dumped him to marry his cousin. The gossip and rumors were one reason he'd avoided the restaurant and every other restaurant he used to frequent. Maybe there was a new scandal to occupy everyone's mind by now. If there was, Dario hadn't heard it.

He introduced the owner to Isabel. What else could he do? By the way he looked at her, Angelo was clearly sizing her up, comparing her to the beauty queen Dario used to bring to the restaurant. The owner turned on the charm, asking Isabel how she liked Sicily.

"It's beautiful. And I'm just learning some of the fascinating history," she said.

"Dario can teach you more than any guidebook," Angelo said with an approving smile. "About everything. Wine and food as well as history. Yes, you're in good hands."

Dario wanted to tell him she was not in his hands at all. But all he could do was to sit there hoping the man would quickly move on to greet other customers.

But Angelo was just getting warmed up. He told Dario he should stop working so hard and come more often to the res-taurant the way he used to, and bring the lovely American. He suggested various dishes she should try and sights she should see in the neighborhood. A few minutes later he finally left them to their food.

"He's very friendly," Isabel noted. "Is he right about your working too hard?"

"In our business there's no such thing as working too hard. We suffered some losses during the drought and the fungus over a year ago, then grandfather got sick and frankly, I have no choice but to work hard. I'm in charge and it's the season of the crush. Everyone in the wine business is working hard." No one had as good a reason for hard work as Dario. No one needed to fill his days with backbreaking physical labor and his nights at his computer studying plans and projects and making spreadsheets. All that to try to make up for the past mistakes and to forget. Mostly to forget.

"I thought you said true Sicilians were easygoing."

"Most of the time, yes. Some of them all the time. I have an excuse for being different. Also it's my nature and the nature of owning a business. You'll see." If she was sensible and left and went home, she wouldn't have to face the hard work of owning a business.

He ate a tomato, then leaned back in his chair and studied her for a long moment. He'd talked quite enough about the Montessori fortunes or lack thereof. More than she needed to know.

Angelo must have noticed the contrast between his ex-fiancée, the stunning Magdalena, oozing self-confidence and bravado, and the plainly dressed American who sat across from him. Fortunately the name *Magdalena* was not mentioned. If he was lucky he'd get through the whole day without hearing it.

In a strange way it was a relief to be with someone who

hadn't lived here all her life, who didn't know everyone and their secrets from their past. It made him feel a sense of detachment, if only briefly, from his work and his family and the past and the pressures he put on himself.

This woman across the table from him with her red-gold hair and her casual American clothes was a stranger in a strange land. A blank tablet. She'd never seen the Roman ruins or eaten capellini Timballo or tasted Nero D'avola. He didn't want to like anything about her, but he couldn't help admiring her as she experienced these things for the first time. She had quite remarkable dark eyes that lit up at the sight of the old ruins or the taste of a superb wine. He liked it that she had no idea what really motivated him, what had really happened in the past, and if he had his way, she never would.

"You ask a lot of questions, but you keep quiet about yourself," he said.

"There's not much to say. As you know, I have no family except for my uncle, who's dead. I quit my job to come here. If everyone in the wine business is working hard now then I feel guilty taking you away from your grapes. You must have work to do. Perhaps we should leave."

He shook his head. "I work hard so the family can live, but even I don't live to work as you do in America."

"How do you know what we do in America?"

"I read. I've seen movies."

"Really? What have you seen?"

"We were talking about you. You left a job behind, anything else?"

"A rented apartment. Some friends."

"No boyfriend?" If she had one, there was a chance she'd go back to him.

"No boyfriend," she said brusquely. But a tell-tale flush

colored her cheeks. There was a story there she wasn't sharing. He knew something about that. As much as he respected her privacy, he couldn't help being curious.

"I'm surprised."

"That I'm independent?"

"That you're single at your age. What's wrong with American men?"

"Most of them are married," she explained. "Which is fine with me. Since I prefer being on my own." She looked down at the table, studying the silverware. Why did he have the feeling this was a painful subject despite her smooth explanation? Or it could be she found the flatware fascinating. Whatever it was, she recovered quickly and looked up, her face composed, her gaze steady. "I could ask you the same thing. If you're not married, why not? What's wrong with Italian women?"

He choked on a bitter laugh. "Ah, there's a subject. Italian women are loud and opinionated. Once you meet some of them you'll see." Fortunately she'd never met Magdalena, and she never would, because she'd moved to Milan. "They have power and they run the families. My mother can attest to that. She and my father are currently in Palermo to take care of some business. So my grandmother is running the house while Nonno recovers."

He stopped his speech about women when the waiter appeared to bring them a bubbling dish hot from the oven called Pasta Alla Norma, a combination of eggplant, tomatoes and ricotta cheese.

"Who was Norma?" she asked.

"The heroine of an opera by Bellini, Sicily's most famous son. Do you like opera?"

"I don't know, I've never seen one. What's it about?"

"Norma is in love with a man who's thrown her over for someone else. But she gets revenge. She ruins him and has him sentenced to death."

"Good for her."

"Except at the end, she jumps into the funeral pyre and dies with him."

"I prefer happy endings."

"So does everyone, but that's not life." If she didn't know that by now, she'd led a charmed life. "You'd like *The Marriage of Figaro* or *The Barber of Seville*. Or something by Puccini. Be sure to see an opera while you're here on vacation. Preferably a happy one."

"I don't think I'll have the time or the proper dress. And I'm *NOT* on vacation."

She was so predictable. All he had to do was refer to her temporary status or her departure and her cheeks turned pink and her eyes flashed as she glared angrily at him. He watched her high spirits and discomfort, knowing he'd caused it.

Taking his time he let his gaze wander from her face to her neck to her arms and breasts and tried to picture her in a formal evening gown at the opera. He was so engrossed he almost didn't notice the waiter who was offering an after-lunch drink from the bar. He shook his head and continued to muse about his companion. She just might enjoy a night at the opera. She certainly had the confidence to try new things. That much was clear. Under other circumstances, he might have offered to take such an attractive woman to the opera since there was absolutely no danger of his ever losing his head and heart to a woman again. He could see her dressed up and gauge her reaction. But she was right, she'd probably be too busy struggling to make a go of it to see an opera. How futile it was, how maddening that she wouldn't take his advice.

If her stay was as temporary as he hoped, she wouldn't be around for the opera season. The sooner she realized she should leave, the better. She'd never make it through a winter on that mountain. Never. As much as it was in his interest to send her packing, it was also the best thing for her as well.

Feeling more confident about the outcome, he signaled the waiter to order two cannolis and coffee. If she had any memories of Sicily when she returned to the States, he wanted them to be pleasant ones—of sightseeing and delicious food and wine. Not of cold nights and frost on the vines. It was the least he could do in exchange for his land.

"Are you sure we have time for this?" she asked.

"Of course. Everyone deserves a day off now and then. We're hard-working when we have to be, but in Italy everyone always has time to eat. And then we'll see some other properties I think you'll like."

She opened her mouth to protest, then closed it, realizing, he hoped, that there was no point in arguing. Maybe she was finally seeing the light. She didn't insist that she had no use for a new house with a solid roof and a clean kitchen. But he knew. He knew that she had a stubborn streak a mile wide. He knew she would initially refuse to consider any other property than the one she'd inherited. But he was just as stubborn.

In the meantime he watched her savor the creamy ricotta filling of the rich pastry. A tiny piece of crisp dough stuck to the corner of her mouth. It was all he could do to keep from reaching across the table to brush it away with his finger. Before he could make a move, she licked her lips and he felt his pulse accelerate wildly. What was wrong with him? Maybe his family was right when they said he'd been working too hard. He hadn't given a single woman a second look since

Magdalena had walked out on him over a year ago, let alone buy them lunch at his once-favorite restaurant. That was all that was wrong with him.

CHAPTER FOUR

ON THE WAY BACK to the town of Villarmosa, Dario showed Isabel several other villas, all attractive, all with intact roofs, some with gardens and others with patios. Isabel very politely but firmly told her guide she wasn't interested in any of them.

"Not interested?" he asked, sounding incredulous. She had the feeling he thought she was deliberately trying to thwart him, as if she was a bourgeois crass American who had no respect for fine living and no appreciation of his culture. He tilted his head to observe the frescoes on the ceiling of the next house he took her to. "The art work here alone is worth the price of the place."

She took a deep breath and tried once again to explain. "I'm sure it is. But it's not my art work. It didn't belong to my uncle. The house has no vines, no grapes, no challenging new career for me to undertake."

"But there is a pond and this one comes with swans instead of water snakes."

She sighed and glanced out the window. It was a lovely picturesque pond with graceful white-plumaged birds paddling by.

"Swans mate for life, you know," he said.

"Even in Italy?"

"Especially in Italy. Divorce is legal here, but not as common as other European countries. For one thing we marry late or not at all and most young people live close to their parents."

She nodded. How cozy it all sounded. How different from the families she'd lived with—single mothers, absentee dads and too many children on welfare. He was watching her to gauge her reaction to the house.

"This house just doesn't speak to me," she said at last. It was true. It was a nice house, the frescoes were beautiful, the swans a definite plus, but she couldn't see herself living there.

He might have rolled his eyes. Whatever he did, he effectively conveyed his dismay at her lack of good sense.

"What did you expect the house to say to you?" he asked, his voice tinged with sarcasm. "*Benvenuto?* Welcome? Make yourself at home? Glad you could make it?"

"I don't think you'll understand, but I need to feel something, a family connection, a feeling that I could live here, that I could belong here."

"Which is what you feel at the Azienda?" he asked. There was no mistaking the disbelief in his voice.

She nodded, but she knew that to him the Azienda was a terrible mess. It really didn't matter what he thought. She'd allowed him to show her around and now he had to do what he'd said he'd do for her.

To her great relief, after three more villas, each one desirable with assets like a deep well and a sturdy roof and even some furniture, he gave up when he saw her negative reaction. She kept her remarks to a minimum and her tone firm, and he finally drove her back to the hotel. She couldn't help feeling victorious. She'd successfully resisted his best efforts and now he owed her.

He walked her up to the door of the hotel and thanked her politely for accompanying him. He was probably furious with her for not caving in, if the frown lines between his eyebrows were any indication, but he said nothing.

Surely even he, incredibly rich, well-connected and sinfully handsome, didn't always get his way? She thanked him for lunch and the sightseeing, then she waited but he said nothing else. He just turned and headed for his car.

"I believe we had a deal," she said, raising her voice.

He looked back at her, seeming surprised. Could he really have forgotten? Not a shrewd businessman like him. He was hoping *she'd* forgotten.

"You said if I didn't see anything I liked, you'd help me find the workers I need."

"And I will. Of course. It may take a little time."

"I don't have time. My grapes are ripe. They need to be picked." She was only guessing. What did she know about grapes really? When he didn't contradict her, she had a feeling she was right. Those grapes were ready and so was she. She couldn't miss this harvest or she'd be behind a year in her quest for a new career.

"I'll see what I can do," he said. Then he got into his car and drove away without a backward glance. She stood there wondering if she'd ever see him again. He was disappointed that his plan hadn't worked. No, he was more than disappointed. He was angry. He couldn't believe she was still holding out on him. She wondered if he'd really keep his promise.

If he never came back, she'd have to scour the town, begging for workers in her broken Italian with the possibility she'd hired a crew of thieves and jailbirds. She needed his help. Badly.

She hated that feeling of being needy. Of depending on someone. It brought back the familiar empty feeling in the pit of her stomach she'd had when she moved from one house to another. From one family to another. No place to call home. No one to turn to. No one who cared about her.

She'd thought things would be different here. Her own house, her own business. She'd be in charge. No landlord, no boss. Instead, she was more vulnerable than she'd ever been.

She was too restless to hang around her hotel room studying her Italian audio tapes or reading how-to books about winemaking. All those chapters about yeast cells and tank-fermentation only made her feel more insecure and nervous about the future.

She took a shower to cool off, changed clothes and headed for the village to look around. For all she knew there might be a group of day laborers standing on the corner looking for work the way they did back in California. She put her Italian phrase book in her pocket, grabbed her camera case and walked the half mile to town down a road lined with lemon trees and almond groves. With the sun low in the sky, the air was deliciously cool.

Villarmosa wasn't a big town. Centered around the town square was everything one needed for the simple life. She took a few photos of the small, leafy park in the center of town and the cluster of old houses around it. Then she walked over to look at an ancient stone church, passed a post office, a garage and a handful of shops, one of which was a greengrocer's where the bins outside were filled with colorful cherries, ripe peaches and juicy melons.

The lawyer's office was located above a small café. She glanced up at the windows where she'd gotten the news about her inheritance, but the shades were drawn and it looked deserted. Maybe her uncle had been Signore Delfino's only client. She didn't see a single worker on any corner asking for jobs.

Her first stop was at a brightly lighted food shop with a

mouthwatering display in the window. Small jars of anchovies and sun-dried tomatoes were flanked by tall, hand-blown bell-shaped glass jars filled with colorful marinated vegetables. Figs, dried apricots and dates were strung like necklaces and hung from the ceiling. Isabel snapped some more pictures, then hung the camera around her neck.

There was no way she could walk by and not go in for a closer look and maybe even a small purchase. Even though she'd had a large and delicious lunch, her mouth was watering and she couldn't resist. Immediately behind the window was the counter where a portly man in a beard and a white apron was slicing prosciutto in paper-thin slices, carefully laying a piece of wax paper between each slice.

The air was redolent with the mingled scents—cured meats and flavorful cheeses. The whole place was like a shrine to the god Epicurus and she'd never seen anything like it. A bell rang when she opened the door and every customer turned to look at her, the new girl in town. Of course, her camera marked her as a tourist, but who was she going to fool anyway? She smiled tentatively.

While she waited in line she studied her phrase book to see how to ask for a small amount of what she wanted. When it was her turn she pointed to the prosciutto and the salami and two kinds of cheese as well as a carton of tiny black olives, and she even spoke a few well-chosen words of Italian.

Feeling proud and pleased with herself for her first foray into town, she followed one of the small old ladies dressed in black out to the street. The woman was bent over with a string bag in hand. Suddenly the bag broke and a half dozen peaches and a jar of honey went rolling down the brick sidewalk.

The woman let loose with a shriek, followed by *"L'oh il mio dio! Che cosa sono io che vado ora fare?"*

Isabel scooped up the slightly bruised peaches and the honey, which was still intact, from the smooth stone walkway, put them in her own camera bag and handed it to the woman, who beamed at her and said, *"Grazie cosi tanto. Siete molto gentili."*

"Prego," Isabel said.

Before Isabel could come up with another appropriate phrase in Italian, the woman waved frantically to someone in a large black car who pulled up and helped her into the back seat. Isabel stood watching as the car, the woman and her camera bag all drove away. Maybe she'd see her again some day or maybe not. Anyway, it was just a case she'd lost. Her camera was hanging around her neck.

Then she proceeded to the greengrocer where the woman must have bought her fruit. The produce was all beautifully arranged, piled high in a cornucopia of spiky artichokes and tomatoes, shiny purple eggplant and pencil-thin asparagus. She took more pictures.

She wanted to buy everything in the colorful display, but she had no way to carry anything else since the old lady had taken her bag. Never mind. She could always come back tomorrow and do some more shopping.

Back at the hotel she decided not to eat dinner in the dining room. Her room came with breakfast and dinner included so she looked at the menu and ordered that night's special dinner. She asked to have it sent up so she could eat in her room and not feel self-conscious about sitting alone while all around her were couples or families.

Just the idea of saying "Table for one" or "I'm alone," sent a lonely chill through her body. Why subject herself to pitying glances from other happy diners? She just couldn't face it, not after the day she'd had. Even though she'd had a good time seeing the sights and eating the food, she'd been afraid to let down her defenses for so much as a minute. She was afraid Dario would pounce on her and make her an offer she couldn't refuse.

Though everyone she'd met here had been nice—except for Dario Montessori and the lawyer—she didn't have the energy to sit down in a room full of strangers and try to make conversation in Italian with the friendly waiters. Here in her room she could relax and get back to studying viticulture and irregular Italian verbs.

First she had a long soak in the claw-foot tub, scrubbing with a sponge and some lemon-infused soap, letting the tension that came from verbal battles with her tour guide melt away. She took her *Guide to Sicily* with her into the tub and read a chapter about "Flora and Fauna." What she read there surprised and annoyed her so much she almost dropped her book in the hot water.

There was a knock on her door. Dinner already? She'd relaxed so much she'd lost track of time. She might have even dozed off, since she was still on California time and suffering from delayed jetlag. She slipped into the plush terry-cloth robe the hotel provided, wrapped a large towel around her wet hair and went to receive the tray from the maid.

Instead of the maid, it was Dario Montessori standing there, this time wearing a leather jacket, straight-leg denim jeans and brown leather loafers without socks. All of which she managed to take in despite the shock of seeing him there outside her door. It was easier and safer to focus on his expensive Italian clothes and shoes than on his craggy face half in shadow, half lit by the overhead fixture in the hall.

"What are you doing here?" she asked, tugging on the lapels of her robe. Why had she opened the door without asking who was there? She could only blame it on her sense of security here in this small hotel in this small town. Now that she realized it could have been a serial killer outside her door, she felt her face turn red with embarrassment. What must this man think of her? Not only did she appear to be a clueless heiress, but she was so naive and trusting she'd opened her hotel door without question to a stranger.

"I came to bring back your bag," he said while his gaze took in the wide-open lapels of her robe. "My grandmother told me how you saved her peaches and her honey. She said to thank you very much."

"Your grandmother? I had no idea. How did she know…?"

"That it was you? She didn't. But your name is inside the case."

"Oh," she said weakly trying to take it all in while she clutched at the front of her robe with one hand and tightened the towel around her head with the other. His grandmother was obviously the tiny little woman in the store.

She didn't invite him in, but Dario stepped inside the room anyway. "I have some news for you about your workers," he said, taking a small leather notebook from his jacket pocket. He must have noticed she wasn't dressed for company, but he didn't care. How typical of him to pursue his own ends and ignore whatever got in his way.

Purposefully he strode past the queen-size bed covered with a pale-green duvet and the antique writing desk, stopped at the round table at the window, took a seat and spread out some papers.

The only thing Isabel could do was sit down across from him as if they were having a business meeting, which they were, except she was hardly dressed or mentally prepared for one. If he'd planned to catch her unawares, and spring some new scheme on her, he'd picked the right time. Her brain was muddled and confused. But her resolve was as firm as ever.

She sat up ramrod-straight in the padded chair and tried to pay attention to what Dario said when all she could think about was how her skin tingled from the bath and how little distance was between the two of them. She felt trapped in the masculine aura that seemed to surround him. There was no way for her to escape or to try to change clothes without looking like a complete idiot. If it didn't bother him that she was wearing a robe and nothing else, why should it bother her? He surely wouldn't stay long.

"I found you a crew of workers." He pushed a list of names across the table in her direction.

"Good," she said. The names were a blur. "Who are they?"

"Old-timers. Men who know their way around the Azienda. They'll be up there tomorrow morning at eight."

"Fine." She breathed a sigh of relief. She might pull this off after all. "How much do they get paid?"

"That depends on their job. Some operate the crushing machine, some the fermenter. They're good men, but you have to be there to supervise them, otherwise they'll take advantage of you."

Isabel blinked rapidly. More men who wanted to take advantage of her? What had she gotten herself into? All she could see was fifty-dollar bottles of Amarado on the shelves without any clear idea of how they got there. She had to keep up a brave front.

"But where…how…?"

"The machinery is in the barn. As far as I know, it still works, but just barely."

"I didn't see any barn."

"You weren't looking. It's there behind the grove of trees behind the house."

"Oh, yes, of course," she said.

"The men expect to be paid in cash. I've written down the hourly rate for each man. Do you have a bank account?"

She shook her head. He must think she wasn't equipped to run a vineyard. Or to make wine. Or to change a tire. But she could learn. And she would.

"You'll want to open an account right away so you can write checks for your utilities. When you get them installed."

"Of course."

There was a soft knock on the door. Now what?

This time it was the maid with her dinner. She came in and set up the plates on the table. For some reason it appeared to be a dinner for two. Had the personnel seen Dario go up to her room and figured they would be expecting an intimate meal for two? Or had he told them he was staying for dinner? Dinner with the one woman he most wanted to get rid of? The woman he'd already had breakfast and lunch with? Hardly.

"Are you staying for dinner?" she asked.

"It looks that way," he said.

No "thank you." No polite refusal. Did he want to stay? Probably not. Then why do it? He must have his reasons. Did she want him to? Definitely not.

Whatever the reason, the maid seemed to know what she was doing, serving veal Madeira in a white-wine-and-mushroom sauce over creamy polenta from a silver chafing dish, along with sautéed fresh spinach. She poured two glasses from a bottle of Pinot Grigio and quietly left the room with a shy smile.

The whole scenario was surreal in the extreme. Was this really Isabel Morrison having dinner in nothing but a robe with the richest and best-looking man in all of Sicily? The same man she'd had lunch and breakfast with? If he shared her sense of the absurd, he didn't let it show. For all she knew, he dined with half-clad women in their hotel rooms every other night. The best she could do was to pretend to be at least that sophisticated herself.

She couldn't possibly change into her clothes at this point, but she did retreat to the bathroom to take the towel off her head, and run a comb through her tangled hair.

Dario looked up when she came back with her hair in a damp cloud of dark-red curls. He swirled some wine around in his glass to keep from staring at her bare legs and the way her robe gaped in front giving him a tantalizing glimpse of one pale breast.

Maybe he shouldn't have barged in this way and invited himself for dinner. It was only now he realized how bizarre the situation was. It had been a long time since he'd eaten dinner with a woman in her hotel room. The first time ever with a red-headed American woman in a robe in her hotel room. And he hadn't planned on her being a distraction, but she was.

The situation had its advantages over the expensive restaurants where he usually dined and where he might have taken her if he'd wanted to have dinner with her. No one but the night clerk knew he was here in her room. Also, he had to admit that any gown she might have worn for dinner would not be as sexy as this robe which covered most of her body, but left him free to imagine what was underneath it.

"I have to say they serve a decent wine," Dario said, tearing his gaze away from her for a moment. He really hadn't meant to stay for dinner. He'd only meant to hand over her camera case, thank her for helping his grandmother and tell her he'd hired some workers. But seeing her with the towel over her head looking like what he imagined a concubine in a harem would look like, had set his senses reeling.

Maybe it was the seductive smell of the soap that clung to her skin that had such a strange effect on him, or maybe he was losing his mind. He told himself to go, to get out of here before he did something stupid, but the voice in his head wasn't very loud or insistent. So then he told himself to shut up and relax.

No getting around it; Isabel looked very different from the enemy he knew she was. Instead she looked soft and warm and very feminine. The kind of woman you wanted to wrap your arms around and get into that queen-sized bed with. The kind of woman whose skin looked so soft and inviting you wanted to taste and touch it. If she wasn't who she was, and if he was someone else, he might be tempted. In fact, he *was* tempted.

How could this red-haired woman who knew nothing about winemaking, wearing only a bathrobe, be a threat to him or his family? She couldn't possibly be. She was as good as on her way home. He felt the guard he kept up around his heart and soul start slipping away. And why not? How threatening an adversary could she be? None at all.

So he stayed for dinner. And allowed himself to look at her between bites of the food, which looked delicious and probably was, but he didn't seem to be able to appreciate it the way he might have if she'd been a plain fifty-year-old spinster, which is what he'd hoped for when he'd heard about her inheritance.

It was late. He was hungry. The veal was tender and the sauce appeared to be exceptional. At the family home the talk would be all about the harvest which could be repetitive after a while. Truthfully, he hadn't seen much of his family in a long time. For one thing, his sisters always had some unmarried woman friend they wanted him to meet. He'd explained over and over why he wasn't interested, but they kept trying. Then he disagreed with them about the same issues, which they rehashed over and over. They just couldn't understand why his working so hard now was his way of making up for his past mistakes, so he gave up trying to explain and just tried to keep to himself. Having someone new in town, even someone he didn't want there but who needed his help, was like an unexpected shot in the arm.

Here was a woman who knew virtually nothing about wine, his family or their problems. He felt as though he'd been dropped down into a little part of America. He felt stimulated and refreshed and challenged for the first time in months. What had happened? Was it just her?

He saw no harm in having dinner with her. All he had to do was play along with her plans for a few days, a week or two at most. He'd even help her pick her grapes and make her wine. When she realized how hard it was and that it wasn't going to work, she wouldn't blame him, she couldn't. She'd just accept the fact she wasn't cut out to be a vintner, sell him the property and go home where she belonged. No hard feelings.

"I'm not sure how this happened," she said, indicating the food on the plates at the table.

"Did you order dinner in your room?"

"Yes, but just for me. I had no idea…"

He shrugged. "I stopped at the desk and asked for your room, maybe they thought…"

"I see," she said. But she looked confused. Maybe she thought he'd told them to make it dinner for two. If he'd known her skin was glowing, her toenails were painted pink and she was fresh from her bath and smelling like a fragrant essence of sweet-smelling herbs, he might have. What was the harm in dining with an attractive woman once in a while? No strings. No obligations. No anxious sisters asking him for a report: *Did he like Signorina X? Did he want to see her again? And if not, why not?* This was just dinner. A business dinner actually. It didn't happen that often. Not to him. Not anymore. Not since Magdalena.

"The food here is quite good," he said. As if that was a good enough excuse for him to stay. "Why would you want to move to the Azienda? No hot baths, no bathrobes. No sauces." He allowed himself still another frank yet leisurely look at the shapely body across the table from him.

"I told you—it's my home and I intend to live there. I didn't come here to stay in a hotel, however comfortable it is."

"Your home isn't quite set up for cooking either." That was the understatement of the year.

She looked around. "I'll miss the comforts here, but I don't need them. I want to live like the natives do. I believe there's a fire pit outside near my pond. I'll have picnics and cook over an open fire."

"Speaking of the natives, my grandmother is very grateful to you. She told me that you chased her peaches down the street for her. She didn't get a chance to thank you properly so she wants you to come to dinner at the house tomorrow night."

"Does she know who I am?"

"I told her." He paused. "You said you wanted to meet the neighbors. Here's your chance. Are you coming or not?"

"Well, I…yes, sure. Please thank her for me."

She poured more wine into her glass and then his. All of a sudden she'd become the hostess. Just as she had earlier today at the Azienda. He could have sworn a few minutes ago she'd wanted nothing more than to get rid of him. She probably still did, but now she was being polite.

"You said there was a long story behind your losing the Azienda," she asked. "What is it?"

CHAPTER FIVE

ISABEL knew he probably wouldn't answer her question no matter how many glasses of wine he drank. After a lifetime in Sicily he was probably able to drink wine all night and still keep a cool head. But she thought it was worth a try. Something must have happened. Something important enough that he didn't want to talk about it.

He probably thought it was none of her business. Maybe he was right. On the other hand, since she was going to live there on the property, with him as her neighbor, she wanted to know. He lifted his glass and considered the wine as a connoisseur would do. Or was he considering spilling the whole story? She held her breath. She waited. He still said nothing.

Finally he drained his glass and set it on the table. "It's not a very interesting story. But since you asked, here it is. Two years ago, I was engaged to a woman. It was, how do you say? A whirlwind time. We traveled from one end of the island to the other. Magdalena was Miss Sicily and she had appearances to make. Festivals to attend. We were wined and dined everywhere, Magdalena was treated like royalty, which she enjoyed and the truth of the matter is I forgot about work. Forgot about making wine. Forgot about checking the vines and following the weather forecast. Which meant I neglected the vineyards just when they needed my help most—during a drought and an infestation of fungus which attacked the plants."

He stopped suddenly. "I'm talking too much. Making excuses for myself. Trying to explain when there is no explanation and no excuse. The rest of the family were working round the clock trying to save the harvest, but I was gone enjoying myself. I let myself be distracted just when I shouldn't have. The result was a near disaster. A blight. The workers hadn't been paid. We had to raise money and quickly. We sold the Azienda to your uncle. All I can say is I regret the whole affair. I regret everything about it. And I assure you it won't happen again." He said the words with so much finality, she had no doubt he meant them.

He stood abruptly and looked down at her. "There you have it. I've talked too much and I hope I haven't bored you. Now I must go. It's late and you have a big day ahead of you."

"I'm looking forward to it," she said, while a million questions came to mind. What did he mean *it won't happen again?* Was he referring to the sale of the land or to getting engaged? What happened to the beauty queen Magdalena? Where was she now? Who broke it off and why?

She stifled the urge to ask these questions. He'd already said more than he'd intended. Instead she said, "It's the first day of my new life as a winemaker. And, by the way, if you ever want to swim in my pond, feel free. Because there are no water snakes in Sicily."

"Is that right?" he asked. A flash of something that might have been recognition of her knowledge of flora and fauna flickered in his eyes.

She stood and reached into the pocket of her robe for the book she'd been reading and opened it and read, "'Sicily's only poisonous snake, the viper, can be found in the forests and flatland in the south of the island.' As far as I know this is not the south of the island and the viper can't swim."

"I never said I was a herpetologist. I'm a vintner. I was trying to warn you about possible poisonous reptiles. For your own good," he said.

For her own good! She doubted that very much. She brushed past him and held the door open.

"Good luck," he said. Then he stood in the doorway, one arm braced against the door frame. He looked at her with a gleam in his eye as though he was about to say or do something, so she waited. And waited. The tension rose. Her cheeks were burning. The temperature in the room must have gone up ten degrees. His gaze held hers and she couldn't look away. All the breath had left her lungs. She couldn't stand there much longer. She had the strangest feeling he was going to do something rash like kiss her. But that was ridiculous. He didn't even like her. Finally after an eternity he seemed to switch gears, change his mind and the gleam in his eye disappeared.

"Thanks for dinner," he said briskly. Then he was gone.

Isabel closed the door and staggered backward. What was wrong with him? What was wrong with her, imagining him kissing her? Maybe it was a Sicilian custom, after dinner you kissed the hostess. Or at least thought about it. It would have meant nothing if he had kissed her. But he hadn't. She was not disappointed. She was relieved.

The next day she needed all the luck she could get and she didn't get much. First she went to the bank, but it wasn't open yet, so she proceeded straight to the Azienda. There, the foreman, whom Dario had assured her was the best in the business, was emerging from the wine cellar, and she suspected that he might have been sampling her vintage collection. At least he was cheerful which was more than she could say for the crew who all looked so glum she thought they must have just lost their best friend.

If only she could talk to them, but whenever she practiced her Italian on them, they just looked at her with a blank expression on their faces. Even without a common language she understood that the old trailer they found in the barn had a flat tire and without it they had no way of loading the grapes as they picked them.

The men handed her the tire and it was obvious they expected her to fix it. Or have it fixed. Fortunately she'd paid attention when Dario changed her tire, knowing he wouldn't always be around, and knowing she was too proud to impose on him again. She located an old spare tire in the barn then took the tools from the trunk of the car and after enlisting one of the workers to help her hold the tire in place, she actually replaced the old tire.

She might have imagined it, but she thought the workers looked impressed. It didn't matter. What mattered was that she'd done it herself. She needed supplies in town so she got in her car and headed down the hill, a feeling of pride swelling inside her.

But that feeling didn't last. One backward glance told her the men were glad for the lack of work. They were standing in her driveway, some leaning against trees, others lying on the ground as if they'd already had a hard day. They wouldn't mind if she never came back as long as they got paid at the end of the day, which would be difficult without a trip to the bank.

She remembered what Dario had said about keeping an eye on them or they'd take advantage of her, but what could she do? She was only one person, one person who had way too much to do and no real knowledge of how to do it.

In the small gas station she asked the owner for a tank of propane and a container of diesel oil. She was pacing up and down in front of the station as she waited when Dario drove by in his convertible. He pulled over and took off his sunglasses.

"Everything going well?" he asked. He must be working, but he looked as though for him it was just another day in paradise, and he didn't have a care in the world. Maybe some day she'd have the same calm, cool attitude, the same confidence, but right now she was frazzled, worried and nervous. And seeing him like this, all she could think about was his almost kissing her last night, even though he hadn't, and she knew it would have meant nothing if he had.

"Fine," she said briskly. Never show anxiety. Always project confidence. Never trust or rely on anyone but yourself. Lessons she'd learned early on. "Except for a few glitches."

"Glitches?"

"Problems." Sometimes she forgot he didn't know every American slang word. "Like the trailer had a flat tire."

"And…?"

"I found another and I changed it myself."

She bit back a little smile at the way his eyebrows shot up in surprise. He hadn't thought she could do it.

"I watched you, remember?" she reminded him.

"Good for you. You're a fast learner."

She blinked. Was that another compliment?

"The men all show up?" he asked.

"Yes, but they have nothing to do while I'm here doing errands."

"Nothing? What about picking the grapes and putting them into baskets?"

She gritted her teeth together. Why didn't she think of that? Because she didn't know there were baskets. She'd changed a tire, but there was more to be done. Much, much more.

"Yes, of course," she said. "That's what they're doing." She didn't think they were doing anything, but she didn't want to tell Dario that. Didn't want him to think she had a problem in the world that she couldn't solve. Didn't want him to think she couldn't manage her hired help by herself. Or at least command respect.

"I'll stop by and see what's happening," he said.

"You don't need to go up there. I have everything under control." She didn't want him acting as if he had the right to take over her job. It was her place and if she needed help, she'd rather get it from someone else. Someone neutral who didn't have something to gain when she failed.

"I'm going to the bank, then I'll head back up the mountain," she added.

"You haven't done that yet?"

What did he think she was, a robot?

"I did go, but they weren't open yet."

He shook his head as if he couldn't believe how stupid she was not to know the banking hours of a small-town bank in a strange country. She'd like to see him in America, challenged by the language, hiring a crew, moving into a house that needed repairs and starting a new business. That would be a very satisfying scenario—to watch him struggle with something…anything. Just a dent in his self-assurance—which bordered on arrogance—would improve her disposition. Just to know she wasn't the only one who made mistakes.

"While you're in town, you might want to negotiate with the company to turn the power back on, if you want electricity, that is. If you do, you'll need to run a wire from the nearest line. And pick up a tank of propane so you can use your stove."

"I'm just waiting for it now."

If he wanted to overwhelm and confuse her and make her

think she couldn't handle it, he was not going to succeed. Because she could and she would. The main thing was to let him know she was on top of everything.

"I don't need electricity just yet. I'll get some candles and I'm sure I'll be fine without lights for a while," she said loftily.

"And will you be fine without running water? You'll need diesel oil for the engine that pumps water to the tank from the well."

"Of course I know about diesel oil," she said, waving a hand at the pump. "I'm getting some here."

She had planned to skip the problem of running water because she'd buy a case of mineral water, but if he found out it would shout "spoiled American heiress" to him. She did want to live off the land if possible. "And I know I'll need electricity eventually."

"Only if you're really planning on living there."

"Oh, I am."

Some day she'd have everything under control just as he did. She'd have water and power and a roof without a hole in it. She'd be making prize-winning wine. She'd have friends and neighbors over to wonderful dinners cooked on her propane-fired stove. She'd invite local people who actually liked her and didn't resent her presence. And she'd smile at people instead of glaring at them, and she would refrain from telling them what to do. In other words she'd be the opposite of Dario Montessori.

He looked at her as if he knew what she was thinking, as if he knew she was dreaming a dream that would never come true. As if he knew she was going to fail and he'd be there to pick up the pieces. She tried to come up with a matching self-satisfied look, but she didn't have it in her. Not now.

The mechanic came out with her gasoline and propane and when she turned around Dario was gone. Then she headed to the bank. No problem there. They were open and glad to receive her money and open an account. It was a different story at the power company which was located above the bank in a small dusty office. There they didn't speak English and quoted what seemed an enormous amount of money. Maybe they didn't understand. All she wanted was a new connection or the old one repaired. They brought out several file folders with her uncle's name on them and had a long discussion in Italian.

Then they shook their heads. Maybe they'd come through. Or maybe she'd have to come back again. In the meantime she'd use bottled water and candles and propane. Her ancestors didn't have electricity and they survived. Of course, she wanted to do more than survive. She wanted to make a fine dessert wine and become part of this community. She wanted to be independent but not lonely. Would all these wishes come true? Or were they just impossible dreams?

When she got back to the Azienda, the workers were strolling leisurely up and down the rows of vines picking grapes and tossing them into baskets. That much they'd done on their own. But if they had to work this slowly it would take weeks to get her grapes picked. She consulted her dictionary and tried out a few commands, indicating that she needed them to work faster and harder.

When she lifted the heavy cylinder of propane out of the trunk of her car, suddenly one of the workmen appeared. They might not respect her, they might not understand her every word, but in Sicily chivalry was not dead yet. She pointed to the house, and he carried the tank to the kitchen where he left it next to the stove, which still tilted to one side. She motioned to the worker to lift up one corner of the cast-iron stove and she stuffed a piece of wood under the leg. It was now level and he left.

Now what? She studied a diagram on the side of the tank. Then she carefully attached the hose from the back of the stove to the cylinder. A picture of a valve with arrows showed her how to turn it on—and presto. She held the sparker to jets and they sent out blue flames. She jumped back from the stove, just in case.

It was magic. She had gas. She stood staring at the gas jets, smiling to herself as if she'd performed a miracle. She had. She could cook now. She could do anything.

She turned off the gas and went back outside, where she grabbed a basket and a knife and started picking along with the workers, hoping to set an example of speed. She set an example all right. She cut her finger and had to open one of her precious bottles of water to wash the cut. At noon the men all stopped working and pulled out huge hunks of bread, wedges of cheese, bottles of wine and slices of meat. They sat under a tall oak tree and spread out their food as if they were picnickers having a day in the country. Isabel hadn't thought to pack a lunch or buy any food. She had a working stove but no food to cook on it.

She was hot and tired and hungry. She longed to take a dip in her pond to cool off but she had no swimsuit and there were all these strangers there. When she saw Dario pull up in front of her house she sighed. She didn't want him telling her what to do and how to do it, so she kept picking and pretended she hadn't seen him.

"Hungry?" he asked when he met her head-on in the dusty row of vines.

She glanced up as coolly as possible. "Not really," she lied while her stomach protested. She'd never admit she couldn't manage her life without him, though she was dying to show off her newly working stove. "I have too much work to do to stop and eat." *And I have nothing to eat.*

"You need to drink something at least. And you need to pace yourself in this heat. You're not used to it. You look tired."

There's nothing like being told you look tired to make you *feel* tired, which is what happened—she was suddenly exhausted.

"I stopped at a farm stand and picked up some food. Stop and take a break." It was more an order than a suggestion and she didn't take orders well, she never had. If her back weren't aching and her forehead weren't pounding, she might have told him to take his food and leave her to pick grapes. But she didn't. Not with her stomach in knots and her throat parched. She wiped her hands on her pants and followed him to his car where he took a large box out of the front seat and walked with her around the back of the house to the overgrown patio with the ancient outdoor fire pit.

Setting the box on the weather-beaten picnic table in the shade of an old tree, he poured ice-cold sparkling water into real glasses. No paper cups for this Sicilian aristocrat.

Isabel sat down, took a long drink of water. "That's delicious," she murmured. Then she looked up at the spreading branches of the old tree for the first time. "Could that be a sycamore?"

"Here we call it a *platania* or plane tree. In the old days the bark and leaves were used for herbal medicine," he said as he uncorked a half bottle of chilled Montessori dry white wine. "Very useful. They even made fabric dye from the roots."

Isabel appreciated the information about the shady old tree, *her* shady old tree. It seemed Dario knew everything about everything. But it was the food that caught her attention. There was grilled lemon chicken fragrant with olive oil and rosemary and cubed provolone and marinated fresh mozzarella cheese. There were small tomatoes still warm from the vine. He set a small container of sweet roasted peppers and another of pesto sauce on the table. It seemed like an endless supply of gourmet items, each one better than the last. Finally there was a loaf of crusty ciabatta bread still warm from the oven.

"Where did you get all this?" she asked, tearing off a hunk of bread to eat with cheese.

"Here and there," he said with a casual wave of his hand. "Besides the farm stand, the bakery and the *deposito* in town. It was on my way."

"You shouldn't have," she said. "But I'm glad you did. I didn't realize how hungry I was. Thank you."

He sat across the narrow table from her with a look on his handsome face she couldn't decipher. It was partly curiosity, partly just landowner whose obligation was to feed the needy. Or maybe what he was doing was force-feeding the goose before it went to slaughter. After all, he surely hadn't changed his mind about wanting her gone.

"I owe you after you shared your dinner with me last night," he said.

"Oh, that," she said, as if she'd forgotten. There was no way she could have forgotten him after he'd left last night. She'd lain in bed picturing him standing there in the doorway, wondering what had gone through his mind. She knew what had gone through hers. She'd wanted him to kiss her. Just to find out what it was like to be kissed by a macho Sicilian. That's all. Today her mind was clear and she was glad he hadn't. She didn't need any more complications to this already awkward situation.

"Yes, that. Sorry I barged in on you."

She shrugged. What was she going to say? *I liked having someone to eat with, even if it was you. There's a side to you I didn't suspect—I'm surprised. That you fell so hard for a woman you neglected your duties. She must have been quite a woman. Why do I think of her in the past tense? For all I knew she's back in the gatehouse waiting for you with open arms.*

"Where do you usually have lunch?" she asked innocently, sipping the cold dry white wine he'd poured for her.

"Sometimes with the workers in the fields," he said. "Or I go home."

Aha, so she was there. "To eat with your family?" Isabel held her breath waiting for the answer.

"No."

That was it? Just no?

"They make a big deal of lunch. And dinner goes on for hours. No matter how busy they are. They want to talk. My sisters want to pry into my personal life. Make suggestions. In Sicily there is no concept of a personal space. I haven't got time for it."

Yet he had time to eat with her? The one person he'd like to see on the first plane out of here? Isabel dipped her bread in the fruity olive oil. Talking seemed to be a Sicilian pastime. And a nice one. Talking and eating fresh local food. She reminded herself not to pry any further into his personal life the way his family did, though of course that was exactly what she wanted to do.

"What's funny?" he asked with a frown on his face. It seemed she hadn't smothered her smile quite enough.

"Nothing. I'm very grateful you made time for me. I confess, I was hungry and envious of the workers with their lunches. I was feeling pretty sorry for myself when you showed up. Everything is wonderful. Delicious." She speared a chunk of ripe juicy melon with a fork he'd provided.

"What about tonight?" she asked. "Won't you have to spend time talking to your family at dinner?"

"My grandmother requested my presence tonight because of you, and no one says no to Nonna."

So he didn't want to be there. He was only going because he had to.

"Maybe I shouldn't have picked up the peaches and the honey for her if I've made things awkward for you."

"Dinner with my family will be a cultural event you should experience. I guarantee they'll be pleasant to you, more than I've been, in any case. And you'll see what Sicilian hospitality is like. Now I should be going. Grapes and more grapes. We only have a short time to get them off the vine."

Isabel got up, feeling guilty for sitting in the shade eating and talking and drinking wine and almost forgetting her problems—one of which was now standing across from her. Another was her house, literally falling down around her and then there were the vines and her workers.

She should never have spent all this time having lunch with Dario. He had work to do and so did she. But it felt so good to relax for a short time with the best-looking man in Sicily, maybe in all Italy and have him feed her with wonderful food and feed her mind with miscellaneous facts and opinions. A guidebook to Sicily can only teach a person so much. A Sicilian with impossibly blue flashing eyes, broad shoulders and a jaw of steel made every word he said about her adopted country seem fascinating and important.

He left the rest of the food, wine and water with her.

"Still no electricity?" he inquired.

"Not yet. I was concentrating on the propane and hooking up the stove."

"Who did that for you?"

"I did." A proud smile tugged at the corners of her mouth. She *was* proud of herself. "One of the workers carried the tank in for me, but I hooked it up. You're right, I do need electricity, but…I can only do so much in a day."

"You've done quite a lot," he said thoughtfully.

It was a good thing she was still sitting down because this too sounded suspiciously like yet another compliment and there were just so many a girl could take all at once.

"You still need to keep your food cold. I'll have some ice delivered," he said. "I'm sure the icebox hasn't been used in years, but it ought to keep things cool for a few days at least."

"Thank you," she said. Why was he being so nice? Must be the Sicilian hospitality kicking in whether he wanted it to or not. He couldn't help it. It was genetic.

Dario spoke to her workers picking grapes on his way to his car, asking them how the work was going. He wanted to be sure they were not taking advantage of Isabel just because she was a foreigner. Or because she didn't know what to expect from them. He was reassured when they indicated respect for her—her ability to try to communicate with them, and her willingness to work along with them.

He couldn't help being impressed too. No woman he knew would pick grapes herself, hook up the propane tank, change a tire or take on a dilapidated house. She'd managed to do it all so far. Maybe, just maybe she'd succeed here where her uncle had failed so badly. There was a look in her eyes that told him she wasn't an ordinary woman. Maybe the best thing for him to do now was to help her when he could with workers, ice, advice and food and back off about pressuring her to leave.

He had no idea what had made him talk about Magdalena last night when he hadn't so much as spoken her name in months. That was one reason he didn't join the family for dinners or just drop in at the house the way he used to. Somebody would always bring up his ex-fiancée. They wanted to know if he was over her. They knew what had happened. The whole town knew what she'd done. Of course he was over her. Did he really have to spell it out? Wasn't it obvious he'd moved on with his life?

The family tried to be tactful, but they wanted a sign that he was no longer carrying a torch for the beauty queen. A sign like taking up with a new woman. No question of that. Instead of stalling or changing the subject or out-and-out telling them it wasn't going to happén or it was none of their business, he chose to avoid the family and their questions. It was easier for him that way, easier to forget.

With Isabel there at dinner, they'd all be on their best behavior and the subject of Magdalena would not come up at all, God willing. Actually it would be good to see the family again. He'd missed his nieces and nephews. He'd always enjoyed their high spirits and their energy whether in a soccer game or a ride on the tractor at the vineyards. But work had been a good excuse for dropping out of sight as much as possible, even if the kids didn't completely understand it, the adults did, or should.

The family liked entertaining. They'd probably like meeting Isabel and would welcome her to the community. After all, they had no regrets about losing the Azienda, they all just accepted it as part of the ups and downs of the wine business. And they didn't understand why he felt so strongly about it. What was the use of trying to explain? So he didn't.

He wondered what would have happened if he hadn't brought the lunch today. Would Isabel have kept working until she collapsed?

If he knew her, that's exactly what might have happened. She was that determined to prove she could do it on her own.

He couldn't just stand by and watch her faint from hunger or get dehydrated. He drove slowly back to his crushing station, thinking about her while he passed acres of ripe grapes, golden wheat waving under a hot cloudless sky and gnarled olive trees. It was possible that she actually deserved this property after all. That was a revolutionary thought, but one he couldn't shake off.

By the end of the day, despite the break she'd taken for lunch, Isabel's back was stiff, her fingers were numb, her neck and arms were sunburned and she'd barely filled one basket. When the men looked into her basket they shook their heads. Of course she couldn't compete with them. But she had to try. She had to show them she wasn't a spoiled American heiress. They quit promptly at five o'clock and asked for their money. As soon as she'd paid them they piled into the back of a truck and they were off to spend their earnings. She envied them.

She realized just how much she was looking forward to a long soak in a bathtub and a change of clothes. And how when she moved up here she'd be roughing it. No hot baths, no clean clothes. She'd give herself one more day. She'd wallow in luxury a little longer, then she'd move up here. She could do it. She could make her little house comfortable. As soon as the grapes were picked and crushed, she'd get busy on the house. She'd make it look like home. Put it back in shape—the shape it must have been in long ago. She could picture it being a blend of old-fashioned charm and modern improvements.

When the ice was delivered all the way to her ancient icebox, she felt a wave of gratitude toward Dario. He didn't have to do that for her. Now she was that much closer to moving in. She opened another bottle of sparkling water, then she went back to the hotel.

She had no idea when and where she was expected for dinner at his family's home or who would be there besides Dario and his grandmother. She hoped it would be a big group, because with a large family his presence would be diluted. Sitting across the table from him, eating bread and cheese and drinking wine at lunch while bumping knees from time to time was enough for one day. He made her uneasy. She wasn't sure why he was being so helpful when it went directly against what he wanted.

He was too big, too strong, too Sicilian, too confident, too sure of himself and of course too good-looking. How could any woman resist him? He and Miss Sicily must have made a striking couple. She'd been part of a couple once, but no one had said they were striking. But that was because no one knew they were together.

Isabel wanted to make a good impression tonight. Not just because these were Dario's relatives, but because they were big landowners, they'd been here for generations and they were her neighbors. She pulled out of her suitcase the one and only dress she'd brought with her, a blue-green cotton sundress with tiny straps and a slim skirt. Was it appropriate? Her nerves were getting to her. Her imagination was running wild tonight. It was fatigue, it was worry and it was him. She was seeing entirely too much of someone she wanted to avoid and who wanted to avoid her. She could only hope his family would show her the famed Sicilian hospitality he'd promised.

Dario went to the hotel at seven to pick up Isabel. The sun was low in the sky and the air had cooled a little. He paused at the front desk and asked if the *signorina* was in. She was. Now that the dinner was looming, he almost wished she'd turned down the invitation for some reason, then he could avoid the scene completely.

He'd made his position clear to his family. As far as he was concerned, there was only one way to make up for losing the land and that was to get it back. But he hadn't considered that Isabel could possibly deserve the land as much as he did. Now, after seeing her toiling away as he'd never seen anyone work, he wondered. Maybe she did.

He had the clerk call up to Isabel Morrison's room and say he would be in the bar waiting for her. He couldn't risk another face-to-face encounter with her in her robe. He'd sworn off women, all women, after Magdalena had walked out on him, but he wasn't made of stone. That much was clear. Then what had possessed him to bring her lunch today? Simply repaying her for the dinner last night. After all, Sicilians had never let their enemies starve, whether they were Phoenicians, Normans, Vandals or American heiresses.

At that moment he looked up when Isobel entered the bar. She looked stunning. The total opposite from the last time he'd seen her only hours ago at lunch, her face sunburned, her hair damp, her face dripping perspiration. Tonight she looked as though she'd stepped right out of an American movie in a turquoise-colored dress that set off her fiery red hair. A more amazing transformation from disheveled and frustrated vineyard worker to glamorous woman he'd never seen. His gaze met hers and held for a long moment while he just stood and stared. The voices in the bar faded.

He'd planned to maintain whatever distance was necessary, however much he admired her determination, that's all he wanted to admire, but at that moment all his plans were forgotten as he appreciated her for what she was, a stunning apparition who stood out even in a crowd of attractive Italian women at the bar. It was her copper-colored hair, and it was her body wrapped in a blue-green dress that showed her curves to everyone in the bar. They turned to gawk at the newcomer. They'd have to be blind not to notice her.

He noticed too. In fact it was impossible for him to look away. In her face he saw hesitation, a hint of unease. After all, she was the stranger here. He had to force himself to stay where he was instead of rushing over to her and claiming her as his guest, or whatever she was. Certainly she wasn't his date, since he didn't date and didn't intend to.

"Ready to go?" he said, and set his empty glass on the bar before leading her outside to his car.

"The hotel owner is very nice," Isabel said as Dario opened the car door for her. "He was telling me about the big wine competition coming up. Sounds exciting and quite important."

"That's right." She wouldn't have any wine to enter this year. She'd be a spectator. She'd see Montessori recapture the gold this year, if the judges knew what they were doing. And next year? Would she be his competitor then?

"I suppose you'll enter."

"Of course. It's important to take away a medal, the gold if possible."

"I'd like to enter. Maybe next year..." She looked away with a dreamy look in her eyes. "Oh, and he told me I need to have a Blessing of the Grapes ceremony."

"That's true." Once her grapes were blessed there was no turning back. She'd be hooked, she'd have respect, a place in the community and she'd never leave no matter what happened. Maybe it was time to recognize the facts and get on the train before it left the station without him.

As he drove he was struck by the sweet smell of jasmine. Just when it was best to keep his distance from her, he wanted to get closer. He wanted to inhale her skin and find out where the scent came from. Was it her bare shoulders? Her neck, her throat? Or was it the flame-colored hair that brushed against her shoulders? He shouldn't have had that drink in the bar. He needed his brain and all his senses on the alert for this evening with his family.

For so long he hadn't looked at another woman. He had a permanent pain in his chest where his heart was and he had vowed never to be taken in again, a vow that was easy to keep. He hadn't been tempted. Not once.

He told himself there was no chance it could happen again. Magdalena had aimed a spear right through his heart. Every time he took a deep breath, every time he woke up in the night thinking of his colossal mistake, he felt the pain in his chest, and he didn't expect it ever to go away. Why should it? He deserved it. It was a constant reminder of how naive he'd been to fall for someone like her.

The American woman was a slight diversion, which he needed. Nothing major. There was no harm in admiring her for what she was or in helping her out when she needed it. His family was right. He'd been working too hard. He needed a break from time to time. Whether sparring with her or feeding her or admiring her determination, he found Isabel a change from his all-work-and-no-play lifestyle. That was all it was. No need to worry. He told himself to give it a rest.

"I'm glad you enjoyed speaking to the hotel owner. The hotel bar is a gathering spot for the neighborhood, which is another reason I strongly recommend you stay there." Why should she deprive herself of the comfort of the hotel and brave the rigors of living at the Azienda?

"You have a point," she said. "I've heard a lot of neighbor-hood news there."

He wondered exactly what she'd heard. Gossip traveled fast in a small town. He was glad he'd already told her his story, and she'd heard it from him. He normally hated talking about his past mistakes. But last night was different. Maybe it was the wine talking, maybe some long-repressed desire to get his story out from where it festered inside, and lay it on the table. It was a chapter in his life he wanted everyone to forget. Especially himself. But so far it stuck like a bone in his throat.

Isabel shifted in her seat and her skirt pulled to one side giving him an extra-good look at her beautiful long legs. He dragged his gaze away. Wasn't there temptation enough without her legs on display?

"I have nothing against the hotel," she said. "But as you know I'm in the middle of an important process and I should be up at my vineyard 24/7," she said. "By the way, I'm very grateful to you for the lunch and the ice."

"Lunch there is fine, but I wouldn't stay overnight if I were you," he said. "Apart from the lack of running water and electricity, there is always the threat of wild boars."

Her eyes widened. Then she turned to give him a skeptical look. "Are they worse than the poisonous vipers in the pond?" she asked pointedly.

"Much worse," he said without apologizing for his white lie about the snakes. "They come at night in packs and uproot your vines."

"Then I'll just have to move up there so I can scare them off," she said.

"Good idea," he said. Obviously she didn't believe him after the snake story. He believed she should be warned, if she was planning to stay up there after dark. Then he shot a skeptical look at her. "How exactly were you going to do that?"

"How do you do it?"

"I use a shotgun."

Isabel pressed her lips together to keep from telling him he'd lost his credibility with her after the snake story. She refused to let him scare her, though the thought of a bunch of wild boars rooting through her vineyard caused goosebumps to pop out on her arms. That and the thought of using a gun. She knew she could never shoot an animal, even if it was destroying her crops. She felt a shiver of fear go up her spine. Just how big were these boars? When should she expect them? How *would* she scare them away?

"It seems," she said as he pulled away from the hotel, "that considering the threat from these wild beasts to my vines, I should definitely be on the site, I mean to move there permanently as soon as possible. What if they come rooting while I'm not there?"

"Hire a night watchman?" he suggested.

"I'm not going to spend money hiring someone to do something I can do myself," she said. "I can tell you are not used to seeing women change tires or hook up their propane stoves. Or scare wild boar either."

"I'm not. I admit it. I look forward to you facing off the wild boars. I have no doubt you'll send them running for their lives."

"I appreciate your confidence in me," she said with a matching touch of sarcasm. He didn't think she could face a wild boar without flinching, and truthfully she didn't either. But she'd never admit it to him.

First she'd give it a try. After all, she'd spent a lifetime standing on her own two feet and learning not to depend on anyone. She didn't want him to think she needed him to help her. He'd already done enough what with the lunch he'd provided, and the ice and the workers he'd sent up.

Thanks to him, so far she'd met some friendly people and

enjoyed talking to them. There would surely be other friendly people as soon as she had some leisure time to circulate and socialize. She felt encouraged for the first time in days.

"Are all your friends in the wine business too?" she asked.

"More or less," he said. "Are all *your* friends in the design business?" he asked.

"No, not at all. And I'm not in the design business anymore. I'm in the wine business."

"I thought you were going to design a wine label for yourself?"

"I am. And I'll design a new one for you too, if you change your mind."

"Go ahead," he said.

"Really? You'd give me a chance? I don't know if you'll like what I come up with, but since you've been so helpful to me, showing me around the countryside and everything and bringing me a picnic lunch, I owe it to you."

She didn't know why he'd changed his mind, but she was glad he had. Her mind was spinning with ideas for a new, enticing label for him. Her fingers itched for a paper and pencil to get started.

After a long drive toward the outskirts of town, she said, "I've been thinking about moving to the Azienda right away. You're not just trying to scare me away with the story about the boars are you? Are they really a threat?"

"They really are. Not every night. Not every season. But it's only fair to warn you. They're fairly large with no enemies. They'll eat everything in sight, especially the roots of your vines."

"What about people?"

"They love people, especially fresh, newly arrived Americans."

She gasped and he gave her a rueful half smile. He was teasing her! That was a good sign. And totally unexpected.

"Which is why if the boars come and rip you to shreds while you're out defending your vines," he continued, "no one will know. The workers will find nobody there in the morning. Then the whole community will blame me for not telling you about them. It's not just the boars. There's that hole in your roof. What if the rain fell through the hole in the roof, you contracted pneumonia and had to be airlifted out to a medical facility? How would I feel then? I'd be responsible for not warning you."

"Thank you. I stand warned on both counts," she said. She hoped he wasn't back to being serious. She shot a glance in his direction but his expression gave nothing away.

"Why do I have the feeling that the minute I was airlifted out of here, you'd be there on the tarmac waving to me with the deed to the property for me to sign over to you?"

He smiled again. Twice in one night. Maybe he was human after all. Tonight when he'd met her in the bar, the smoldering look he'd given her had made her feel hot on the outside and shivery inside. She wasn't sure how to interpret it.

"You may not believe this," he said, "but I'm beginning to think you have what it takes to make it there after all, despite the boars, bats and the hole in the roof."

"Really?" Her eyes widened. A warm feeling suffused her bare shoulders and crept up her neck to her face.

"Don't get me wrong. I'd still like to see the land back in our family, but I'm willing to help you fight off the pests because maintaining the vines is important to me. I can see you appreciate the place almost as much as I do. But you have to get a telephone so you can call me if anything goes wrong."

"That's very generous," she said. "But I couldn't impose. You've already done enough for me."

"I just want you to know I've been honest about everything I've told you. I don't know everything. I *thought* there were poisonous snakes in the pond. I was wrong. It's not the first time. Go ahead and swim there."

"I will," she assured him. "Just as soon as I buy a swimsuit." It was a good feeling knowing she'd won his respect.

"What about you?" he asked. "Haven't you ever been wrong about anything?"

"Wrong? Oh, yes. I've been very very wrong. And I've made my share of mistakes." She pressed her lips together. She'd come all this way to get away from the past, why go into it now? But instead of keeping it to herself, she found she couldn't stop talking now that she'd started. "I trusted someone I shouldn't have. After all the things that happened to me in my childhood, all the disappointments, all the moving from family to family, despite all the dashed hopes that I'd find a home and a family, I still let myself believe someone loved me…." Her voice trembled and she stopped and took a deep breath wishing she hadn't blurted out the part about love.

"Nothing. It doesn't matter now." That was a lie. It still mattered. It shouldn't but it did. It mattered terribly. She'd fallen in love, given her heart away when she knew better. It was the last straw. "It taught me a lesson. More than one. I won't make the same mistake again. But it led to my coming here and starting a new life. The inheritance from my uncle came just when I needed it the most. It was a godsend. Do you believe in miracles?"

"No," he said shortly.

"I don't either, but why, just when things looked the bleakest, did my uncle leave me the vineyard? Doesn't that sound like a miracle? If it isn't, I don't know what else to call it."

He didn't say anything, and she wondered if she'd talked

too much about miracles and getting the Azienda. Of course he didn't believe she'd received it in the form of a miracle. He believed she'd received it because her uncle was a failure as a vintner. She just wanted him to know how much her inheritance and coming to Sicily meant to her.

He turned off the main road and onto a long lane lined with cypress trees and ending at a magnificent white stucco house. It was like a travel poster with Come to Sicily written on it and it took her breath away. She'd never seen anything so beautiful and so inviting. The fragrance of heavy-laden orange and lemon trees filled the air. Late-afternoon shadows fell across the lane.

"Your house?" Why did she even ask? Of course it was.

"My family's house. Very old and lived-in."

"So they don't know who I am?"

"I told my grandmother. She knows."

CHAPTER SIX

IT WAS more than a house. It was an estate with gardens, patios, outbuildings, cottages and one beautiful main house. Isabel had known it would be nice. She hadn't known it would be a dream house straight out of *Italian House Beautiful* magazine. It was surrounded by citrus trees and twisted ancient olive groves. It had everything an Italian villa should have, including the children who came running from all directions, playing with their large shaggy dog and shrieking as if they hadn't seen their uncle Dario for years.

They threw themselves at him, and he hoisted one little boy onto his shoulders. Two others grabbed his legs and tried to hang on. Isabel stared at the sight of the man she would have voted "most likely to avoid children and animals."

She couldn't be more surprised to find that he was so popular with this group. And he apparently liked them as much as they liked him. So he wasn't always all about business. He'd said he didn't live to work. Maybe it was true.

If anyone had asked her, she would have sworn he was a loner, in fact hadn't he as much as told her so? She assumed that because he kept to himself and avoided his family, he wouldn't want to play or laugh with anyone, including kids or dogs. How wrong she was. His deep laughter echoed in the summer air. It was a rich, warm sound that left her dazed, standing there alone with her mouth open. Dario, children and pets. She couldn't have been more surprised to see them all together, getting along famously.

A short pretty woman in a simple but well-made blue cotton dress and leather thonged sandals intercepted Dario and the children.

"Dario," she said, hugging her brother. "You came."

"Of course I came," he said. "Nonna's orders." He turned and waved to Isabel. "Isabel Morrison, this is my sister Lucia."

"Welcome to El Encanto," Lucia said.

By then the children's entreaties were getting louder. Dario excused himself and he and the kids walked across the lawn.

Lucia watched her brother go. "I'm so glad you could come to dinner. I can't believe Dario came too." She was still staring off in the distance as if she was afraid he was an apparition, and if she took her eyes away, he'd disappear.

"But I thought…"

"You thought we all ate together every night like a big happy Italian family? Some of us do, but Dario has been absent from family gatherings ever since…for a long time. We have you to thank for bringing him here tonight."

She sounded truly grateful, as if Isabel was responsible for Dario's presence when it had been his grandmother's orders that brought him.

"Thank you for inviting me. Your house is lovely."

"It's old and been in the family for generations. Come and have a tour. You'll have to excuse Dario for taking off, my children are so excited he's here. They haven't seen much of him lately. As I said, his visits are rather rare."

"I understand the crush is keeping everyone busy," Isabel said.

"We're all busy," his sister said, a frown creasing her brow. "But we still make time for family. At least the rest of us do."

Isabel didn't know what to say. Fortunately, Lucia filled in. "It's the children who miss him the most. He's always been their favorite uncle and they don't understand where he's been and why he doesn't come around to see them. Do you have children?" she asked.

"Uh, no. I'm not married." Why did Italians think every woman her age should be married?

"I see. Well, they've dragged my brother off to have a look at the new tennis court and they'll try to persuade him to play a game or two with them. When it comes to the children, he's their hero and there's no one else they'd rather see. He's *Babbo Natale,* our Father Christmas and Paolo Maldini, our most famous soccer player, rolled into one. Though I warned them he is busy and might need to leave early tonight they just don't understand. They only remember when he'd come by just to see them. He hasn't been the same…for quite a while."

Isabel was certainly getting a new perspective on Lucia's brother. He didn't seem like the type of man children would adore or drag off to play tennis with. And yet, according to his sister, who ought to know, he was. He'd told Isabel his family was too intrusive and demanding. Maybe it was more than that. Or less. Maybe it had more to do with his former fiancée.

Lucia led Isabel through the heavy oak front door into the house with its brightly tiled floors, comfortable couches and antique pieces and into the kitchen. There, standing on a stool so she could reach the stove, and stirring a pot of sauce was the old woman she'd met at the market. She looked up and smiled broadly.

"Ciao. Benvenuto alla nostra casa."

"Grazie per ivitarlo," Isabel said.

The grandmother let out a torrent of Italian words directed to her daughter while Isabel stood and admired the kitchen with its rough red-tiled floor and the brass pots and pans hanging from the ceiling.

"She says she hopes you like Sicilian food."

"I'm sure I will. Does she do all the cooking here?"

"Oh, no. We have a cook who's been with the family for years. But she oversees it all, the sausage stuffing, the rolling out of the pasta, making the cheese that comes from the goats my grandfather raises. And when we have a special guest like you, she has to be right here in the kitchen to make sure everything turns out right. Actually my family and I live nearby but we love coming for dinner at least once a week. So did Dario once. Before he became a workaholic."

"What a nice custom," Isabel murmured, ignoring the part about Dario and his work habits. She knew if she had a grandmother and a big family she would be here once a week at least. But then she hadn't been through a drought and a fungus attack and the sale of her land as well as a personal problem like a broken engagement. Maybe he just needed time out from his family. Since she had no family, it wasn't easy to imagine. It certainly sounded like he'd been avoiding them for some time.

One day she would have a tradition like this. She wouldn't have grandchildren, but she could have friends. She could have a garden, maybe even a goat or two. She already had a pond and a vineyard. She had more than most people she knew.

"Come and see the garden. Nonna is very proud of her Romano beans, eggplants, figs, zucchini and Italian chiles. But the roses are all Nonno's. Before he had his stroke he poured all his energy into them. I'm sorry you won't meet him tonight. He's having dinner in his room. He overdid it today, and he needs rest."

Stepping outside through a lovely shaded patio with hanging pots of bright geraniums, Lucia took Isabel to the garden and pointed out the different types of roses her grandfather had planted. "These are Balkan double yellow, over there pink Queen Isabella. Your namesake," she said with a smile. "They almost take the place of grapes in his life, but not quite."

"He must have plenty of grapes as well. Your Montessori Cabernet and Merlot wines are famous. Dario told me he is especially proud of—what was it? A Benolvio we had at a restaurant."

Lucia gave her a surprised look. "Where was that?"

"I don't know the name of it, it was an old palace at one time, I believe."

Lucia nodded. "The Palazzo, yes it's a wonderful restaurant, a special place, I'm glad he took you there. And surprised. He always tells us he has no time to spare."

"This was actually more of a business lunch," Isabel said, hoping she hadn't spoken out of line. "I have a lot to learn from him about growing grapes and making wine." She was sure it was a business lunch as far as Dario was concerned. He'd never have taken her to lunch if he hadn't been trying to get her to buy another property instead of the Azienda.

Lucia paused and gave Isabel a curious glance, then she picked some lovely pink Queen Isabella blooms. She tore off some faded petals as the heady fragrance filled the air. It was time for Isabel to level with his sister.

"You see, I'm in the wine business too. I inherited the Azienda Spendora from my uncle."

"Oh," Lucia said. "So you're the one."

"Yes, I'm the one." What had she heard about her? That she was unreasonable? That she didn't deserve the property?

Lucia gave Isabel a long look, then she smiled and said, *"Benvenuto in Sicilia."*

"Grazie," Isabel said, relieved at her reaction, so different from her brother's the day she'd arrived. She seemed as friendly as she'd be to any newcomer to the area.

"How did you meet Dario?" Lucia asked

"Not only did he give me directions on my first day," Isabel said, "but he was kind enough to take me to the property himself." At the time the word *kind* hadn't crossed her mind.

"I see," Lucia said thoughtfully. "How nice."

Just then a woman wearing an apron came out and rang a little bell. She spoke a few words to Lucia and Lucia said, "It's time for dinner."

The bell seemed to work well. Children came running from every direction along with several adults, including Dario, who had joined his grandmother and was deep in a serious conversation with her. They made quite a striking pair, the small, black-clothed old woman and her handsome strapping grandson. From the way she was talking to him, it seemed more of a lecture on her part than a conversation. Isabel would have given much to be able to understand it. Anyone who could lecture Dario must be a figure to be reckoned with.

Before he took a seat, Dario greeted his brothers and sisters, their husbands and wives, who all seemed delighted and surprised to see him. They hugged him, kissed him on both cheeks and were peppering him with questions which he interrupted to introduce them to Isabel as the new owner of the Azienda, in case someone hadn't gotten the word. Then he took a seat at the outdoor table under the arbor across from her.

There was no mistaking the looks she got. They'd heard about her and now they wanted to see for themselves. There were somewhere between fifteen and twenty at the table and she had a hard time remembering who was Maria, who was Paolo, which girl was Francesca and which was Angela.

They all talked at once in rapid Italian while the maid served bowls of a light creamy soup. Just one taste and Isabel was convinced she was in heaven.

"Do you like it?" Dario asked from across the table.

"It's wonderful. What is it?"

"*Maccu*, a Sicilian specialty. Made from our own home-grown beans. Grandmother wanted to make a special dinner for you. She's convinced no restaurant or hotel can come up with the true Sicilian cuisine."

"Tell her thank you. I'm very grateful to be included at your family dinner. It's not the same as eating at the hotel."

"Although the food at the Cairoli isn't bad," Dario said with a pointed glance at Isabel. "They make a very decent veal Madeira. They even have room service."

The knowing look he gave her told her he hadn't forgotten the intimate dinner they'd shared. Or not kissing her. She hoped his family didn't think she'd invited him to that intimate dinner, when his arrival had been a complete surprise to her. In fact, he had a disconcerting way of seeming to see right through her clothes, as he did right now, when his intense gaze seemed to strip away her sundress.

She shivered in the warm air and concentrated on the soup in front of her. Did anyone notice this casual flirtation on his part? Or was she mistaken? That was not flirting, Sicilian-style, it was just...something else. Or was it what they expected from him? More likely they had once been used to him bringing women to dinner for the family to meet and scrutinize, at least in the days before his engagement. What did they think of his ex-fiancée?

"Nonna told us how you helped her last evening at the market. I'm afraid shopping is rather limited around here," Angela said.

"Not at all. I bought some wonderful meat and cheese. And the fruits and vegetables we had for lunch today were beautiful," she said to Dario.

His sisters exchanged looks. Maybe she shouldn't have said anything about their lunch. Maybe they'd get the wrong idea, think that she and their brother were spending quite a lot of time together. *It's just business*, she wanted to say. But was it?

"I mean, I'm not yet set up for housekeeping, so Dario brought me some food, or I don't think I could have made it through the day," she said, feeling her cheeks grow hot as she struggled to make less of the lunch than it was.

"How do you like the Azienda?" his sister Caterina asked politely.

"Very much. It needs work, but it has lots of potential."

Again, looks were exchanged around the table. What did they expect? That she was a spoiled heiress who was so discouraged she might turn around and go back to America? Maybe that's what Dario had told them.

Dario said nothing. He couldn't be surprised since he'd heard her say the same thing before. Instead he took a large helping of the caponata, a classic mixture of eggplant, capers and olives.

His grandmother looked around the table at her family who were unusually quiet. *"Que es male? No le gradite?"* she asked.

"It's delicious, Nonna," Dario assured her. He got up and poured red wine from a carafe for everyone. "Isabel is interested in history. Of course Sicily is the ideal place to study the past since we've been colonized for six thousand years by everyone who came sailing in the Mediterranean. I showed her the ruins at Casale since they're close by."

"I thought you were too busy for sightseeing," his brother Cosmo said from the end of the table. "Now we see the reason you suddenly find a time in your schedule for someone, but not your beloved family." He shot an admiring glance in Isabel's direction.

Dario, back in his seat, poured some fruity olive oil into a small dish. "Never too busy to give a newcomer a tour of the countryside," he said.

"And how do you like our wine?" his brother Cosmo asked. "Or should I say *your* wine?"

She reminded herself this was the brother who'd been at the Azienda the other day.

"It's held up well," she said. "I'm no wine expert. But I know what I like. Your family's wines are superb. You must be very proud of them."

When she looked up Dario was looking at her. His blue eyes were deep and unfathomable like the Mediterranean. If he was trying to send her a message, she had no idea what it might be. Maybe it was that she'd said the right thing or maybe the wrong thing. She only knew that his intense gaze sent a tingling up and down her arms and a strange feeling in her head as if her brain was on vacation. She wasn't thinking clearly. It was hard to concentrate. She was glad the adults all spoke English, because it was all she could do to concentrate on saying the right thing in her own language.

His sister Lucia who was at the end of the table with her two children, said, "We've been doing this so long, sometimes we take our wine for granted. That's why the *concorso* is so important."

"The competition. I've heard about it. You're sure to win."

Dario changed the subject. "Isabel is an artist," he said. "And she's volunteered to design a new label for Montessori wines."

"An artist?" Lucia said. "Then she's come to the right place. There are some beautiful scenes to paint here. You must show her Nonno's paintings. The ones you hung on your wall. She'll appreciate them."

"I'd love to see them." Isabel looked around the table at the smiling faces. She'd never felt so welcome before. As a child she'd been used to being shunned by the other kids in her foster families, who were afraid she would siphon off scarce supplies of food and affection. What a contrast to the warm-hearted Sicilians. This new experience made her feel warm all over.

The next course was a crisp grilled snapper served with small new potatoes and fresh-picked asparagus garnished with toasted prosciutto. The children got restless as the meal stretched on and dusk fell over the patio and the gardens. The crush was on, this was a critical time in the vineyards, but this wine family was sitting around enjoying dinner as if they didn't have a care in the world, just as Dario had said they would. But he didn't look as if he was wasting time and wanted to leave. Maybe tonight he'd let himself slip back into the Sicilian way—work hard but enjoy life too. And if by some chance you're not enjoying life, act as though you are.

Maybe some day she'd be able to adopt this lifestyle and have a leisurely dinner every night with friends. Now that she had a functioning stove and ice in the icebox, she was getting closer. If only she didn't have to worry about making wine and making a living. Not to mention the Blessing of the Grapes ceremony she was supposed to host.

When the children got up and pulled Dario up from his seat, he said, "The kids want to play tennis on the new court to try out the night lights." He turned to Isabel. "Do you play?"

"Not very well," she said.

"Then we'll give you a lesson," he said. "Come with us."

Leaving the rest of the family behind, they trooped down a limestone path through the garden, past a grove of olive trees, past a turquoise swimming pool with underground lights, to the illuminated tennis court. It was a beautiful location, surrounded by towering cypress trees and paved with red clay.

One of the nephews handed Isabel a racket and told her to take off her shoes.

"He wants to be your partner," Dario explained. "They all do."

"You'd better tell them I'm not very good."

Dario sent the kids to practice volleying back and forth across the net. "They don't care. My nephew thinks you're pretty. I'm sure you've heard that before."

She hoped he couldn't see her blush in the gathering darkness. "More often I'm told I'm stubborn."

"That doesn't surprise me. Is that why you've never married?"

"No," she said, bouncing the ball against the clay surface. "I believe we've already had this discussion. Maybe I prefer to be single, just like you. For your information, I was engaged once, but it fell through. Why are you so interested in my personal life?"

"Most Sicilian women your age are married. That's all I'm saying."

"In America women marry late and sometimes not at all. Women can be whatever they want. They can live alone or with a partner. Marriage isn't essential for happiness." *If I really believe that, then why did I make such a terrible mistake by rushing into an engagement?* "Maybe you have a more traditional idea of marriage and family."

"Not me. I know things don't always work out. As you see, my sisters are all happily married with children, and no doubt my brother Cosmo will also settle down one day. That leaves me."

"You mean you've given up on marriage?" she asked.

"Marriage is not in the cards for me. Tonight you saw family life at its best. No arguments, no disputes. Everyone was relaxed and having a good time. We're good hosts and you're a good guest. We tried to show how wonderful family life in Sicily can be. And it can. Make no mistake about that.

"Now they're sitting around the table talking about the crush, the fermentation, the bottling and the advertising campaign. There's rehashing of past harvests, going back one hundred years or more. It can get very tedious. It's worse when the conversation turns personal. 'Don't give up, Dario,' they'll say. 'There's the Benvolio girl who's looking for a husband. What about Maria Del Popolo? Or Angelina Spano or…' All I mean is we live in a small world here where everyone's involved in everyone else's life whether they want to be or not."

"As someone who has no family, it doesn't sound so bad," she said. In fact, she'd be willing to accept a little interference in her personal life in exchange for a group of relatives and a small world.

She was relieved when they stopped talking about marriage and family and started a game of tennis. But first there was a dispute about who was playing on whose side, and Dario repeated that all the kids wanted to play with her.

"I thought you were their favorite uncle."

"I am, but you're the new girl in town. How can I compete with that?" he asked, a half smile on his face.

She didn't know what to say to that. Just the hint of his smile had her feeling as though she'd just had the rug pulled out from under her, if they had rugs on tennis courts. It was so unexpected. Is that what the kids did to him? Made him relax and feel young again, even though he said he didn't want to spend time with his family?

Though she hadn't played for a long time, she managed to get in a few good shots that went past Dario. The children clapped and he looked mildly surprised each time she did it, but the next time he hit back with such force she didn't have a chance to return it. If she'd doubted his competitive nature before tonight, she had no more doubts. Perhaps he had the same impression of her. She didn't like to lose, on the court or in the vineyard.

When they pronounced the game a draw, Isabel and Dario walked back to the house behind the children who ran on ahead. "You're not bad. Where did you learn to play?" he asked.

"In high school. I took a tennis class. First time I'd ever been on a court. It was fun. It came sort of naturally. The teacher loaned me a racket and taught me a lot. She said I had a good stroke."

"I'll second that."

"She encouraged me to try out for the school team, but then I had to move. My new school didn't have a tennis team. And I didn't have any equipment."

"Did you move often?"

"All the time. I had to go wherever a family was available to take me in."

"That must have been difficult."

"Not really," she said. "It was interesting meeting the different families, attending different schools, making new friends." That last part was a lie. It was so difficult making new friends every school year, she had finally stopped trying and spent her free time studying and her lunch hours in the library because she knew she'd have to win a scholarship if she wanted to go to college. "I suppose you've lived here all your life."

"I spent some summers away playing sports, even a summer at tennis camp, though you wouldn't know it from my game tonight. Then I went to university in Milan and studied finance. But I knew I could never live there. This is my home."

"Your sister said they haven't seen much of you lately."

"I've been busy," he said shortly. "It doesn't mean I don't care about them. I thought they understood that."

"Family ties are important in America too, it's just that I didn't have any. Which makes it easier for me to move across the ocean and make my home here." It didn't mean she wasn't envious of him. Who wouldn't be? Still, she owned a house and a vineyard, and he wouldn't hear her complain.

When they returned to the house, lights were glowing from every room. Framed in the windows were various family members. Isabel felt a wave of homesickness wash over her as if she had a home to be homesick for.

She missed being a part of a home and a family, no matter how happy she was to have a house at last. She blinked back a sudden tear, grateful for the darkness falling. She couldn't let Dario see even a hint of sadness or envy. She'd been called a crybaby too many times until she learned to control her emotions. No matter how bad the insults or the abuse she'd suffered, she'd learned never to give anyone the satisfaction of seeing her cry.

"I promised to say goodnight to the kids," he said. "Then I must leave. Come with me if you like."

She couldn't help being touched at this gesture to include her. She was also touched and surprised by his relationship with his nieces and nephews. They obviously liked him tremendously, and he seemed to have fun with them. It was a whole different side to him, one that caught her off guard. Maybe she'd judged him too hastily.

At first she'd thought he was a hard-hearted, greedy land-owner who'd do anything to get rid of her and get his hands on her property, but then he'd stayed for dinner in her room, confided in her and brought her lunch when he didn't need to. He'd ordered ice for her instead of letting her food spoil. And now here he was playing with dogs and kids. What next?

The children were gathered in the large bedroom on the second floor for a sleep-over, cousins and brothers and sisters, some perched on their beds, others on a thick carpet on the floor where they'd made room for Dario to sit. The scene was straight out of one of Isabel's fantasies. She wondered if they knew how lucky they were to be a part of this family. Probably not. Most children took for granted being loved and well cared for. She hadn't.

They cheered loudly when Dario came in. He grinned at them. She couldn't believe this was the same man who had glared at her only a short time ago. He took his place while she sat on the edge of a bed as he told them their favorite story which he translated into English for her as he went along.

"The history of our island goes back to thirteen thousand BC," he said. "That's when this land was inhabited by a group of powerful giants who were descended from the god Zeus.

"The giants thought they were smarter and more powerful than the gods. The gods were so angry they banished the giants and sent them to the underworld below the volcanoes to make weapons for them, like thunderbolts. Are the giants still there?" he asked.

"Yes," the children chorused.

"How do you know?" Dario asked.

"We hear them when the volcanoes erupt."

"They're struggling, trying to get back to earth, but the mountains are too heavy."

Just then Caterina came to the door and told the children it was bedtime.

"But he didn't tell the part about how Sicily got its name," her son protested.

"Or how it got to be the bread basket of Europe."

"Another time," Dario said. Maybe he'd finally had enough family time.

The kids moaned and groaned, but before they turned out the lights, one of the children, a little girl named Ana-Maria kissed Isabel good-night. One hundred painful memories knifed through her, of missed hugs and kisses, of bedtimes without anyone to say goodnight to her.

Isabel stood at the door for one last look inside the bedroom. She'd never seen such an idyllic scene. Lamps turned low, children sleepy-eyed and tired from a summer day of play in the sun. She caught her breath and longed for her camera or her sketchpad. Maybe she didn't need it. It was a scene she wouldn't soon forget.

She wondered if Dario ever longed for kids of his own. She'd given up on that dream. It sounded as though he had too.

She went to find his grandmother to say good-bye and thank her. She was in the kitchen sitting in a rocking chair and talking with a woman who must be the cook. Isabel told her in her best halting Italian how delicious the dinner was and how beautiful her house was and how she admired her gardens. The old lady hugged Isabel and said something that might have been "Come again," or "I hope my grandson treated you well," or something entirely different. But the smile on her small round face was unmistakably warm and friendly.

Isabel looked around at the huge restaurant-size oven, the open shelves stacked with old plates and the well-worn chopping block in the middle of the room and she longed for a kitchen exactly like that, laden with memories, handed down from generation to generation.

She wanted to have bread rising on the stone counter, and smell the yeasty fragrance. She would do it. She would make the kitchen at the Azienda such a place. Smaller of course, and without any family mementos, but it would be all hers.

When his sisters came into the kitchen carrying coffee cups, she thanked them for their hospitality. Impressed by their friendliness, Isabel took a seat on a stool at the counter.

"I've had a wonderful time tonight," she said. "I hope next time I can invite you to the Azienda."

"You mean you're going to stay there?"

"Yes, of course."

"Alone?"

Isabel nodded. She hoped she wouldn't get another lecture on the dangers of wild animals. "I've been alone since I was eighteen. So it's nothing new. Except that now I have a house of my own. I know it's in bad shape, but I plan to fix it up. I have a lot of work to do," she said. "First comes the harvest of course."

"Welcome to the winegrowers of Sicily," they chorused, lifting their glasses in a spontaneous toast.

Isabel felt a rush of gratitude. They barely knew her and yet they'd welcomed her with so much warmth she swallowed over a lump in her throat.

"I didn't know how you'd feel about my inheriting the land that used to be yours. I didn't know what to expect. I'm an outsider. My uncle didn't do much for the place. You have every reason to resent my barging in like this..."

"Is that what Dario told you?" Lucia said, her hands on her hips, a frown on her face.

"Well..."

"We sold the land to your uncle, and it's yours now," Francesca said. "You have every right to it. Dario may have a different opinion…"

"Because of what happened," Maria said. "He lost his heart to that…horrible woman…! Then she…"

"Don't even speak of her," Francesca interrupted, her mouth curved down in disgust. "She is dead to us. Dario lost his heart yes, and the land as well. What of it? It's over. No one blames him. He's Sicilian, after all. We are emotional people. We fall in love and give our all and if we make a mistake, so be it! He'll get over it. Maybe not today or tomorrow, but some day."

Lucia turned to her sisters and announced, "Dario took Isabel to the Palazzo for lunch. It's where he used to take Magdalena, remember? That's a good sign he may be getting over her. I thought he'd never go there again. And he brought you here tonight." She looked around the room at her sisters and sisters-in-law. They nodded vigorously.

"I think that was your grandmother's idea," Isabel said.

"No matter. I believe you must be good for him," Lucia said with a smile. "He needed a distraction. What about you? You're not engaged to someone back in America, are you?"

Isabel was a little startled at their personal question. But flattered too, that they felt they could ask her.

"I was once, but…it didn't work out." It never works out when the person you're engaged to is already married. "Just when I was at a low point and needed a change in my life, I got the letter from the lawyer about my inheritance."

Lucia clapped her hands. "A miracle," she exclaimed.

Isabel beamed. "Exactly."

"Dario can help you with everything," Francesca said. "He knows about making the Amarado wine."

"He can give you Italian lessons," Lucia added.

"He's already helped me more than I expected," she said. "Considering how he feels about the Azienda."

"It's not only losing the Azienda he suffers from," Maria said. "It's what Magdalena did to him."

"He is the oldest son and he feels guilty for what happened," Lucia added. "Too much. He's supposed to look out for us all. But he takes his responsibility too seriously. Ever since, he hasn't been himself. We've moved on. He hasn't. Maybe you can help him forget..." She looked at Isabel with a hopeful smile.

Isabel didn't have the heart to tell her *Maybe nothing*. She was in no position to help Dario forget anything. She was a foreigner alone in the world, still suffering from the fresh wounds of betrayal herself. She was the last person to help someone else recover.

She was going to say goodnight and thank them for a memorable evening when they mentioned the Blessing of the Grapes.

"Your first harvest at the Azienda. You must have one."

"We'll talk to Father Guiseppi. He'll sprinkle the holy water over the grapes."

"The holy water?" Isabel had thought maybe it was just a party, but it sounded like a serious religious ceremony.

"You should choose a date. And it must be soon so the blessing can take effect, and you'll have a good harvest."

Out on the terrace, Dario was talking to his brothers and brothers-in-law. They all stopped talking when she appeared and stood to either shake her hand or kiss her on the cheek and wish her well.

"Don't forget to show Isabel Nonno's paintings. They're very realistic," his sister said. "Even if she's never seen the volcano, she'll recognize it right away."

Dario nodded, but Isabel didn't want to presume on his improved attitude toward her any more. He'd already spent quite a lot of time with her today. He'd come here tonight as a favor to his grandmother and had seemed to have a good time with his family, but maybe he was just putting up a good act to make the evening a pleasant one for everyone, which he had, at least for her. Just seeing Dario in this setting made her evening one she wouldn't forget. He was standing at the door, staring up at the starry sky as if he'd never seen it before.

"What did you think of them?" Dario asked when she got into the car. "They can be overwhelming."

"They were nice. Very nice indeed. I didn't know what to expect, but they're wonderful. They couldn't be more warm and friendly."

"They liked you too," Dario said. "They're impressed with how you try to speak Italian, how friendly you are and of course they like the color of your hair. 'Like the sunset,' they say."

She felt a flush color her cheeks. "That's nice to hear." She took a deep breath. She knew she shouldn't spoil the mood, but she had to know. "I wonder if they like me so much because I'm not Magdalena."

Dario pulled up in front of his house. The car jerked to a stop and he turned to look at her. She met his gaze reluctantly, sorry she'd said anything.

"It's true they didn't like her," he said brusquely.

"They believe she hurt you." Nervous, she turned and stared straight ahead.

"That's not true," he said after a long silence. "I was disappointed, not hurt. No one can hurt you unless you let them. Unless you let down your guard. In my case it was my fault, not hers. I was wrong. I should have known Magdalena wasn't right for me. Everyone else knew. Not me, I was blind. I didn't want an ordinary girl. And she was far from ordinary." There was irony in his tone. Isabel could only guess at what he meant, knowing that she was a beauty queen and was treated like royalty. "I was greedy. Ordinary women weren't good enough for me. I wanted someone different. I wanted her but she wanted more than I could give her. I don't expect you to understand," Dario said. "You're from a different world."

"But I do understand. I was even stupider than you. I fell in love with my boss. He was married with no intention of getting a divorce. I wasn't the first woman he'd romanced while still married. Everyone else knew all about him, but not me."

"Why didn't they tell you?" Dario demanded.

"No one knew we were seeing each other. They had a rule at the company—no inter-office dating. So we had to sneak around, never going out in public, always meeting on the sly. It was exciting at first and I was flattered by his attention. I was a nobody, just one of many, a graphic artist in a big company. He was a big shot, in charge of the whole operation, rich and powerful. I thought...I don't know what I thought," she said, stumbling over her words.

"You thought he loved you," Dario said. This was something he understood. "Didn't you?"

She nodded. "That's what he said. And I believed him. Stupid, stupid me. What was wrong with me?"

"Nothing. Nothing's wrong with you." He reached for her hand and held it between his own. Her fingers were cold and stiff. He would like to meet this rich powerful guy who'd lied to her. He'd like to knock him across the field and show him he couldn't treat people that way, no matter who he was. "You were too trusting, that's all," he assured her. "Sometimes it takes a shock to make a change in your life. You learn to deal with disappointment by moving on. You gain something knowing it can never happen again. You won't ever let down your defenses again."

"You're right. I won't," she said. "Have you really recovered?"

"I'm fine," he said flatly. He didn't want her to think he was still suffering. Or that he'd ever suffered at all. He hoped his sisters hadn't said anything like that. "I know one thing. I will never fall in love again. Not after what I've been through."

She withdrew her hand. He got out of the car, came around and opened the door for her. When she got out he slammed the car door shut.

"Enough of the past," he said as if he was slamming the door on it too. "It's over. Come in. I want you to see the paintings." Dario wanted to change the scene, change the subject and forget the past for a while. Both hers and his. He hadn't meant to talk about Magdalena and he knew it was hard for her to talk about her boss. He could tell by the way her voice shook and how cold her fingers felt.

He seized on the opportunity to show her Nonno's paintings to have something else to talk about. She'd made an effort to get along with his family and he appreciated that. Magdalena had sneered at his family for being bourgeois country people.

He wanted to see Isabel in a different atmosphere, in his house with no family around. No woman had been there since Magdalena, who'd thought it was "rustic," and totally unlivable. If ever there was a woman who was the exact opposite of the pampered city girl he'd been engaged to, it was the down-to-earth American.

His family liked Isabel, but was it true they liked her because they'd like anyone who wasn't Magdalena? They'd been polite and impressed by Magdalena's title of Miss Sicily, but that was all. They thought she was cold and self-centered and definitely not good enough for him. Funny, because Magdalena thought she was too good for him.

Tonight he wanted to see what Isabel thought of his house. She had the most expressive face he'd ever seen. If she thought it was rustic he'd know. Right now she was taking it all in from the desk piled high with bills and paperwork to the over-stuffed chairs and the sturdy coffee table with industry magazines stacked there.

Isabel stood on the hand-woven carpet with the geometric design and looked around. The room was spacious and snug at the same time, with the scent of leather and wood in the air.

Dario switched on the lights and opened the windows. A cool evening breeze wafted into the room. Isabel drew in a quick breath. There was music playing from somewhere. A woman was singing a plaintive song. Even though she couldn't understand the words, she understood the feeling, so familiar, so touching.

"Opera?" she asked.

"Puccini. Do you like it?"

"It's beautiful. But it sounds sad."

"It is sad. Her lover has left her."

No wonder Isabel could identify with the song. "I'm beginning to see it's true that Italians are very emotional people," she said.

"We're also proud and loud and impulsive and passionate." He had an intense look in his eyes that told her he was all of those things, perhaps the reason he'd fallen so hard for Miss Sicily. She, on the other hand, was trying to be sensible. Passion and runaway emotions were what had got her in trouble. She too had learned a hard lesson.

She bit her lower lip and looked away. Too many impressions were all crowding in on her. There was way too much to take in—the kids and Dario, Dario and his family, Dario and his past. She'd seen a different side of him tonight, a softer, caring side he hid from the world. He'd finally opened up about his affair. Just enough for her to guess he'd been hurt, no matter how much he denied it.

A rush of mixed emotions left her feeling shaky and confused. Who was he? What did he want besides making wine, winning wine contests and moving ahead with his life? He'd been a different person tonight. He hadn't mentioned wine or her land at all. Maybe she was different too.

"What a wonderful house you have," she said, tearing her gaze away from him to look up at the rough-hewn timbers on the ceiling and the wide-planked wood floors.

"It's better in daylight when you can see the fields and the hills from the front windows."

"It's nice at night too," she said, admiring the huge picture window and the stone fireplace, picturing a fire blazing there in the winter. Did he and Magdalena spend any time here or were they always on the go?

"I haven't done much to it since I moved in two years ago. Just moved a few walls to make it seem bigger."

The room, with the colorful rugs on the floor and leather ottomans, reflected his personality and his country. She'd never seen him relax, but she could imagine him reclining in one of those big chairs gazing at the view or at a fire on the hearth.

She was uneasy being so close to him, his masculine aura so much a part of him he was oblivious to it, but she wasn't. She was only too aware of the way he towered over her five-foot-ten-inch height, the strength of his grip on her arm, the warmth of his hand when he held hers, his strong features and his equally strong will. She walked across the room to look at some photographs in frames on a high table. They were pictures of a vineyard and people all holding wineglasses with a priest in the center wearing his clerical robe.

"Could that be a Blessing of the Grapes?" she asked.

"From a few years ago, yes."

"I suppose I'll go ahead and have one at the Azienda. I want to do what's expected."

"What's expected is a party for everyone in the village. The priest blesses the grapes, everyone sits down to a large feast and they toast you and the harvest."

She sighed. "It sounds overwhelming. Along with picking grapes and remodeling the house, I'm not sure I could manage a party."

"If you don't, you risk a bad harvest," he said. "It's not that complicated. I'll help you set it up."

"You'd do that for me?" She stared at him for a long moment then turned to look at the paintings. After all, it *was* the paintings she'd come to see. Instead she was getting a different look at a side of Dario that she'd never seen before, and she wasn't sure she wanted to. It was an eye-opening experience to see where he lived and find out so much more about him. What she learned made him more intriguing than ever. It would be better for her equilibrium if it made him look less attractive, less interesting. But it was just her luck he was probably the most attractive and unavailable man in Sicily.

"Your grandfather's very good," she said, walking up for a closer look at the towering volcano and its purple shadow in the picture. "Does he still paint?"

"No. It's too bad. Maybe he'll get back to it when he recovers. He hasn't been the same since he had a stroke."

"He must be an amazing man, making wine, growing roses and painting pictures. I hope I'll get a chance to meet him."

"He'd like to meet you, I'm sure. But I warn you, he doesn't mince words. He speaks his mind. He can be charming when he wants to be. He's always had a weakness for pretty women. It runs in the family." He paused. "Not the charm but the weakness."

Her cheeks burned. Not just at the unexpected compliment, but at the significance of the remark.

He stepped forward, a look in his eyes that made her knees weak. It was the same look she'd seen last night when she'd thought he was going to kiss her.

"I don't know about the weakness," she murmured, "but I'd say you've inherited your share of the charm." Would she have said that yesterday, before he brought her lunch, before she met his family, before she heard what he had to say about his ex-fiancée?

He smiled. A slow smile that spread to his intense blue eyes. Her heart thudded. If he touched her her skin would sizzle. That's how hot she was.

The sound of the Puccini aria rose and filled the air. She didn't know what the words meant, but she understood pure passion when she heard it and when she felt it. Isabel's heart raced. The longing in the song matched the longing in her heart. A longing to hold and be held. To kiss and be kissed. That's all.

He was going to kiss her this time. She knew it.

CHAPTER SEVEN

WHEN HIS LIPS came down to claim hers she was ready. If truth be told, she'd been wanting him to kiss her since the first time she'd seen him when she'd thought he was a humble field worker. His kiss was so hot she thought she might burn up. She felt his arms tighten around her. His strong, muscled thighs pressed against her. She moaned softly, wanting more. Her heart banged in her chest and she kissed him back.

He groaned deep in his throat and pressed her back a few steps to the wall where she could lean against the smooth stones, all without breaking the kiss, even intensifying it. Then the rhythm changed just as the music did. He invaded her mouth with his tongue, taking and giving her so much pleasure she wanted to sink to the floor and take him with her.

He splayed his hands on her bare shoulders. Then he pulled away and looked at her as if he was seeing her for the first time. The cool skeptical look he once wore was gone. Instead there was white-hot desire, burning with a blue flame. He didn't say a word, but the questions in his eyes were clear. Do you want this as much as I do?

She wanted it as much as he did. Needed it. Needed to feel whole again, desirable again, if only for the moment. If only for tonight. She didn't hesitate. She put her arms around his neck and kissed him again. The answer to his unspoken question was hot feverish kisses she couldn't stop. He reached for the strap on her dress and teased it off her shoulder. She gasped and realized he could peel the straps off along with her dress and make love to her tonight on the floor or in his bedroom and no one would find it strange. In fact, maybe the whole family assumed that's what they were doing. They might think it would be good for him. Good for her.

Yes, she thought. Yes. She was alive in every pore of her body. More than that, she felt warm and feminine and desirable for the first time in a long time. It was a heady and delirious feeling. It shocked her, but at the same time she never wanted it to stop.

Dario was like no other man she'd ever known. He was Sicilian. He was passionate and proud and impulsive. He tasted like wine and smelled earthy and masculine and he felt hard and solid. He felt like the kind of man you could lean on. If she were someone else. Or if he were someone else. But he wasn't, and neither was she. She wouldn't and she shouldn't lean on anyone—not on him, of all people. He wasn't in the market for a relationship and neither was she. Just a flirtation. There was nothing wrong with that, was there?

Her breath was coming in short bursts. Her face was flaming. With one finger he stroked the rounded curve of her breast through the cotton fabric of her dress. She could only imagine how it would feel if she could shed the dress and let it fall to the floor at her feet. His hands would caress her heated skin, teasing...soothing, exciting. She didn't want him to stop. She wanted this feeling to go on forever. She wanted to stay there in his arms, to take the next step wherever it led.

Her whole body throbbed with anticipation. But somewhere in the back of her mind she knew she had to stop. With shaking fingers she adjusted her strap, then put her hands on his shoulders and held him at arm's length. She was gasping for breath, trying to fill her lungs with air. Trying to regain her self-consciousness.

"I...I think I'd better go home," she said, only half aware she didn't really have a home to go to. Not yet. "I'm afraid I lost my head for a moment." If only she had a better excuse.

"Nothing wrong with that," he said. "I thought it was about time for this to happen." His voice was so deep and low she had to strain to catch the words. "You're a very attractive woman and I've resisted up until now, but it hasn't been easy. Blame it on the night, the wine or the dress you're wearing. Or blame it on me."

She shook her head. "It was my fault. I know better. Or I should know better. Now I should go."

"Sit down for a minute," he said.

Obediently she sank into one of the leather chairs at the fireplace. Every muscle ached and her skin was covered with goosebumps. He stood with an elbow against the stone mantel, looking down at her. She had no idea what was on his mind. Her brain was racing, trying to anticipate. She was trying not to show how much his kisses affected her. They made her melt inside. They made her wonder if they meant anything to him. She knotted her fingers together and waited. There was a long silence before he finally spoke.

"I have to apologize," he said at last.

"Please don't. I wanted you to kiss me."

A hint of a smile tugged at one corner of his mouth making him look more gorgeous than ever. He leaned forward and focused his intense blue gaze on her. "Not for that. For trying to pressure you to sell the land when it was obvious you have more of a right to it than I do. The important thing is that you want the best for it. I do too. You'll pick grapes and you'll make prize-winning wine. And if you need help, you can call on me. When I saw you on the road for the first time and I realized who you were, I confess I wanted nothing more than for you to leave. I'd been through a bad time since Magdalena left. I'd been betrayed and, what was worse, the whole world knew it. I was angry, not just with Magdalena, but with everyone in the world. With friends who told me it wouldn't last, with my family who warned me she was wrong for me. And most of all with myself for being blind." He shook his head as if he couldn't believe what had happened.

Isabel wanted to get up and throw her arms around him and tell him he wasn't blind, he was just human. He was Sicilian, proud, passionate and emotional.

"For a long time I hid out from my friends and family," he said. "I didn't want to see anyone. I didn't want to be the object of their pity or their scorn. You came along. You knew nothing about what happened. You forced me to take action. At first I did everything to discourage you. I thought you were another opportunist, a gold digger, out to take advantage of our family."

"So you told me there were snakes."

"Snakes, mice, bats, boar…whatever it took. They weren't all lies. But I underestimated you." He gave her a wry smile.

She nodded. "It happens to me a lot. I'm used to it. No one thought I'd amount to anything being tossed about as a child, no parents, no money, nothing. But I got an education, a job and now a vineyard. And I made it on my own. With the help of my uncle of course." Maybe it sounded like bragging; she hoped he'd accept it for what it was—the truth.

He went to the sideboard, opened a bottle of an amber liquid and poured two fingers worth into two glasses. He handed her one and touched his glass to hers.

"To your uncle," he said, "for leaving the grapes to you."

"To you," she said. "For the food, the ice and the workers." *And the kisses. Oh, those earth-shaking kisses.* "What would I have done without you?"

She sipped the rich warm flavor of aged Scotch and felt it burn a trail right through her body.

"You'd be fine. You don't need me. You have what it takes to make things work. You've got more determination than anyone I know."

His words warmed her heart along with the Scotch. But she did need him. Badly. "I have a feeling I'll need all the determination I can get. So far I haven't spent a night at the Azienda or fought off the wild boar—which I'm sure are real. So maybe you should save your praise until I do."

He shrugged. "All right."

She forced herself to stand and look at the door. She had to leave even though she wanted to stay. It was wrong even to consider staying and she knew it. She'd been badly burned and she knew enough to stay away from the fire. Falling for Dario would be the worst thing she could do. Just a taste of having someone to kiss, someone to talk to, someone to share her thoughts with, someone to lean on when things went wrong and someone to share the work with made her want more.

She who prided herself on her confidence, her ability to stand on her own, was feeling vulnerable tonight. Tomorrow she'd be back to her self-reliant personality. She had to be.

The breeze from the open window had cooled her overheated face, the music had died down and she had to leave. He didn't try to stop her. He picked up his car keys and they left the house. She turned to look back, wondering if she'd come back to his house. Wondering if he'd ever share it with anyone. Wondering what this evening meant to him. Maybe it was just a transition from Magdalena to the world of available women again. Maybe she was just the first on his road to recovery. Maybe she was just a bridge, nothing more, nothing less.

For her it was just a few kisses, and some exchanged confidences, that's all it could possibly be. She might be tempted, but she'd never trust, never love and never let her guard down again. Not for anyone. Especially not for a passionate Sicilian who was out of her reach. He'd made it clear he felt the same.

In his car on the way to the hotel, with the scent of roses in the air, she decided to set matters straight now that she was in command of her brain again.

"I have to tell you, after what I've been through, I don't indulge in casual flirtations," she said.

"I never thought you did," he said soberly. "My kissing you was spontaneous and rash. I told you it's a Sicilian fault. It had something to do with the way you look tonight. And the way you play tennis. The way you watch me repair a flat tire. The way you eat melon and drink white wine. All those things made me want to kiss you. And the way your chin sticks up in the air when you're angry. It was an impulse, that's all. At least on my part. I can't answer for you." He slanted a look at her that said he was aware that the kisses they'd shared were not one-sided. "I haven't any other excuses. It won't happen again unless you want it to."

What could she say to that that wouldn't sound desperate? Of course she wanted it to. Of course she'd deny it. She was shaky and tense and on the edge of her seat all the way home in his car. She hadn't meant to get carried away, but what did he expect? He was the sexiest man she'd ever known. He radiated heat and masculine strength in ways she'd never experienced. She'd have to be made of stone not to respond.

What a day it had been. Filled with unexpected discoveries and obstacles, a dinner with sparkling conversation, followed by mutual baring of the souls and emotional upheaval, physical and emotional intimacy and now this. Her mind was spinning and she longed for a hot bath and a soft bed. How would she cope with a hard bed and no hot water? How would she cope with wild boar and an overwhelming attraction to the one man she should avoid getting involved with?

CHAPTER EIGHT

DARIO DROVE as fast as he could on the winding road back to the Montessori estate. He tried to put Isabel Morrison out of his mind, but he couldn't erase the taste of her lips on his, the feeling of her body pressed against his and the touch of her skin, as smooth as silk.

Even though he'd told her and himself it wouldn't happen again, even though he knew it shouldn't, he wanted it to. He wanted to see her eyes full of desire, feel her body tremble in his arms, inhale the scent of her hair, and hear her sigh deep in her throat. Just a taste of her only made him want more. She excited him, challenged him and tantalized him. She made him feel alive again for the first time in a year. Maybe she didn't want a casual flirtation, but he was starting to think that was exactly what he wanted.

She was probably going to stay; he'd come to terms with that fact. The two of them were both young and unattached. They were in the same business. He'd offered to help her. There was no way they could avoid each other even if they wanted to, which he didn't. As long as she didn't expect anything from him except support in the vineyards. That he could give. Anything else—promises or commitments—was out of the question. He'd learned his lesson, as he'd told

Isabel, and learned it the hard way. But an affair didn't have to mean forever. It could mean for now. It could be good for both of them. She needed to forget about the guy who'd treated her badly just as much as he needed to forget about his past, move on.

He dropped back in at the family house before going home. Just to see what they had to say about Isabel. As if he didn't know. He'd seen the approving smiles on their faces before he left tonight. The family had a tendency to jump to conclusions and have him married off before he knew it. Before things got out of hand, it was time he made it clear to them that while Isabel was attractive and admirable, there was no room in his life for a permanent woman, not now, not ever. As for a girlfriend... As for an affair... He was beginning to think that was a different matter.

The family was in the living room, everyone but his nonna, who'd gone to bed. As soon as he walked in the door, just as he anticipated, they started.

"This Isabel is a beautiful woman, Dario. She likes you. Why I don't know," his brother teased. "So what are you waiting for?"

"We liked her. The kids liked her too," Lucia added pointedly.

He knew what she was referring to. The kids hadn't liked Magdalena. And she hadn't liked them. *They're so loud. Always in the way*, she'd said. *Let's not go to the house. It's all about them. So many of them. All the time.... We can never be alone.*

"As far as we're concerned, Dario, Magdalena is gone and forgotten," Maria burst in. "No one blames you for what happened. Let's forget the past and welcome Isabel by helping her with the Blessing. I'll talk to Father about it and we'll all be there to celebrate. It's the least we can do for a newcomer."

"I'm sure she'll be grateful for your help," he said. The

Blessing was fine, as long as they didn't think Isabel was another potential fiancée. There would never be another one of those in his life and he was glad of it. But Isabel was good for him. He'd readily admit that. She'd made him feel as if he'd had a jolt of electric power shot into him. The kisses they'd exchanged had left an imprint on his mouth and his mind. She was obviously what he needed, even though he hadn't known it. An affair, a romance. He had to persuade Isabel that they could have one, and he had to make it clear to his family that that was all it could ever be. Not tonight though. He didn't want to start a discussion about his future, so he said good-night and left before they could continue to sing Isabel's praises.

Back at his house, the living room seemed large and empty. He looked around, picturing Isabel in front of the mantel, seeing her face when she heard the music and imagining her standing there, her dress on the floor, in nothing but briefs and a bra and then…

He was trying to see the place through her eyes wondering how it looked to her. Too severe, too masculine, too subdued?

He saw her as she was, standing breathless, her eyes half-closed, one strap off her shoulder, looking so soft, so desirable… He didn't know what would have happened if she hadn't stopped him. Would she still be here?

Dario fell into a dreamless sleep for the first time in months. He was no longer haunted by disturbing negative memories of Magdalena, instead there were visions of Isabel passing through his subconscious, walking through the vineyards, her hips swaying, her glorious hair shining like copper in the sunlight.

Isabel didn't see Dario or any member of his family the next day. She didn't expect to, but she wondered, would he act as if nothing had happened? Would she? What did the evening mean? Was it the beginning of an affair or the end of their dispute? Or was it both?

The question kept her awake half the night. That and the memory of how his kisses felt on her lips and in her mind. She replayed his words over and over—*an impulse...spontaneous and rash...* Which would mean that it probably wouldn't happen again. The idea left her feeling low. She knew it was wrong, but she wanted more. How much more, she didn't know. How would she handle another relationship? This time she would not get her heart broken. She was too smart. She'd been through too much.

It was good to have a day without seeing him. Even if it seemed like a day without sunshine. But she didn't want to rely on him and she certainly didn't want to think about him all the time. He was an attractive man and a different man from the one she'd met the first day. He'd changed his mind about her and about the Azienda. She'd changed her mind about him.

She hadn't come to Sicily to have an affair with anyone, least of all the richest and sexiest but most unavailable man in the area. He'd already been burned by a beauty queen. He should be off limits. Until last night she'd thought he was. She'd told him that she didn't indulge in casual flirtations. Now she couldn't help but wonder if the attraction between them could lead anywhere, whether a casual flirtation could be better for her than a serious relationship...

She spent the day at the vineyard supervising and picking grapes with the workers, but she kept listening for his car, watching the driveway and trying not to feel let down when he didn't come by with food, drinks and advice. And hot, sizzling kisses that rivaled the sky-high Sicilian summer temperatures.

In the evening she was restless. She decided she couldn't stay at the hotel anymore no matter how much she wanted a hot bath and a soft bed. So she had an early dinner of spicy pasta arrabiata and a crisp salad by herself in the hotel dining room. She was the only customer since most Italians didn't eat dinner until ten o'clock.

She kept her eye on the door but no one else came to eat at that early hour. No tall, handsome Sicilian came looking for her, to join her and share food with her. She ate alone, determined to enjoy it. But what a contrast with her meals with Dario. The hotel dinner at the small table where their knees bumped and she tried to act normally while dressed in a robe, the family dinner where he sat across from her looking like an Italian movie star while she sipped Sicilian soup.

Then she checked out of the hotel before it got dark and she lost her nerve. Without a backward look at the charming Hotel Cairoli she drove resolutely back to the Azienda. It was dusk and the sun turned the fields on both sides of the road to gold.

Tonight the Montessori family would again be gathered around a big table laughing and talking and sharing their experiences with each other. Would Dario be there too? Had he changed his solitary ways and rejoined his family? Or was he eating alone as she had?

Was it a foolish dream to think she'd ever be at home here the way his family was? Maybe after about one hundred years. Should she consider selling the place to his family? Never. In fact, not one of them had even mentioned the possibility. As night fell she couldn't see the broken tiles on the roof or the hole above the bedroom. This was her home, flaws and all.

After scrubbing her kitchen with some of her precious bottled water by the light of a gas lantern one of the workers had brought her, she climbed the stairs to her bedroom, tired, sore and just a little lonely. She, who'd spent her whole life alone, was feeling lonelier than ever.

She lay in the narrow bed that she'd covered with layers of foam and blankets, then the new sheets and more blankets that she'd bought at the dry goods store in town. Too tired and too full of anxious thoughts to sleep, she stared up at the stars through the hole in the roof. It wasn't quite as romantic as she'd hoped it would be. In fact, it was a little scary being alone in the dark, hearing strange rustling sounds from somewhere outside, though nothing, not even wild boars, would let her admit her fears to anyone, especially Dario. Where was he tonight? Probably not at his grandmother's house. Out with friends at the hotel bar? Or back at his house tackling the mountain of paperwork she'd seen on his desk and listening to opera? She tried to forget the sound of the music, the touch of his hands on her shoulders, and the warmth of his lips on hers. Did he know she'd checked out and was staying here at last? Was he thinking of her?

She could blame her lack of sleepiness on the bed or the strange house, but it was more likely she just couldn't turn off her brain.

As for her feelings... They were what was keeping her awake tonight. His kisses had awakened something deep inside her that she had thought was long buried. She knew better than to get carried away by another attractive man, but she wasn't made of granite. She couldn't turn off her attraction for him so easily. He was Sicilian, she was in Sicily and she loved the land, the climate, the food and the people. It would be so easy to fall hard for a Sicilian and jump into an affair for the full Sicilian experience. If she was a fool that is. She finally fell asleep while thoughts of boars invaded her dreams.

Isabel told herself every day that her job and her life would get easier. She told herself not to expect Dario to keep turning up when she needed him. But after a few days passed without him dropping by or running into her in town she began to wonder when she'd see him again—especially at night when she lay in her lumpy bed thinking of what a huge project she was facing, harvesting grapes and making wine by herself.

Her thoughts bouncing around in her brain kept her sleepless night after night. But one night it was more than her thoughts that had her wide awake. There were noises outside, getting louder, a strange cacophony of low growling and grunting. Finally she couldn't pretend it was just the wind in the trees any longer. She jumped out of her narrow bed and went to the window that overlooked the vineyard.

She shone her powerful flashlight onto the field below, and there they were! She jerked up and bumped her head on the window frame at the sight of the big brown animals with short legs and large heads running pell-mell through the vines. She pulled back from the window and rubbed her head.

Every instinct told her to close the window, go back to bed and let them destroy her vines. How could she alone defend her grapes from the wild marauders? And there went her future wine sales just like that. But she had no gun, no crew, no way to scare them off. She could go down there and yell at them, but what if they turned on her with their tusks and speared her leaving her alone and bleeding in the dirt?

She'd sounded brave when discussing the boars with Dario, but that was all talk to impress him. She wasn't brave at all now with the actual animals in sight. The beasts with their dark fur and huge snouts were after the roots on her vines and would destroy her whole crop unless she did something about it.

"Go," she shouted at them. "Get out. Get lost. Those are my grapes." Her voice shook. Her cries were swallowed up in the night air.

Above the noise of the boars, she heard a car. A few minutes later she was blinded by a flashlight shining up at her from beneath her window. She shaded her eyes and saw Dario looking up at her. He had a shotgun over his shoulder. She felt a surge of the same relief a settler in the old West would have felt at the arrival of the cavalry. She braced herself against the window frame.

"What are you doing here?" she asked, as if she didn't know.

"I heard the boars were around tonight. I thought I'd better come by and scare them off," he said.

"I'll be right down."

Barefoot, she hurried down the narrow staircase to meet him at the edge of the vineyard.

"Did you know I was here?"

"I knew you weren't at the hotel. They told me you'd checked out a few days ago. Why didn't you tell me?"

"I...uh...I was busy." That was better than telling him how desperately glad she was to see him. Why hadn't he come looking for her? Because *he* was busy. And she'd had no right to expect him.

She was so glad to see him she had to fight off the urge to throw her arms around him and let him hold her and tell her everything was going to be okay. He was so big, so solid and so confident. He looked as though he could handle any emergency.

"Let's go," he said and led the way to the vineyard. It was like a safari, walking single file behind him, stalking the wild boar while he shot pellets at them. Her heart pounded. Her bare feet hit the dirt that sifted between her toes. Her mouth was dry. It was scary and exciting. Dario would let loose a rain of pellets, the boar would scatter, run and then more would take their place.

Dario explained that though the pellets bounced off their

fur, they stung and the more they shot the faster the boar would run out of the vineyard. After a long hour, the beasts had finally run off and the vineyard was eerily quiet again. It was over. Isabel's knees wobbled and her hands shook even though she'd done nothing but watch and stalk.

"I hope this doesn't happen every night," she said weakly. "Thank you. You saved me. Maybe they haven't done too much damage." It was too dark to see how many vines had been uprooted.

"I think we caught them in time."

He said *we* but she hadn't done anything but yell at them ineffectually from her window.

She glanced at him. Now that her eyes were used to the dark, she could see his dark hair, a flash of white teeth, his wide mouth and his crooked nose clearly.

"I'll have to get a gun like yours," she said. "And learn to shoot it."

"Another day," he said with a glance at her nightgown. She'd almost forgotten she was wearing a long, sheer cotton gown. His eyes seemed to smolder as he surveyed her body. She could feel the heat right through the cloth and she was afraid she might catch on fire from the sparks between them.

The smell of crushed ripe grapes filled the air and a soft breeze caressed her overheated body. She ached to feel his arms around her. She wanted to share the triumph of defeating the wild animals even though he'd done all the work. She had no idea how long they'd been out there. The first rays of sun were creeping over the hills.

Impulsively she reached for his arms and pulled him towards her and kissed him. Kisses tinged with relief and gratitude and something else she didn't want to name.

His arms tightened around her and her body was pressed

against his. She told herself to pull away though it felt so good to feel his heart beat in time with hers. She told herself to let him go. Thanks were enough. Falling for Dario was the stupidest thing she could do. He could never return her love even if she offered it to him. He'd made that very clear.

But the voice of reason was drowned out by the pounding in her head. There was even a buzzing in her ears. She reminded herself she wasn't falling in love. This was not love. It was lust. It was longing. Anything but love. She would never love again. She knew the painful consequences. She knew how humiliating it was to fall for someone who wasn't available. What was happening now was that she was just having fun for the first time in a year. She didn't want a serious relationship any more than he did. An affair. An affair to remember when winter came and there were no more grapes to pick and no more excuse to see Dario. That's all this attraction could become.

His kisses and the look in his eyes made her feel like the bravest and the most beautiful woman in the world. Made her want to rip off her nightgown and run through the vines and jump into the pond with him. Feel the cool water around their bodies.

Finally it was he who broke the kiss and held her at arm's length. He was breathing hard and there was a shuttered look in his eyes she couldn't decipher. "I'd better let you get some sleep."

"Sleep?" She looked around. Sleep was the last thing she wanted. She was full of energy. "It's morning. Would you like some coffee?"

She noted his look of surprise and said, "Follow me."

The air was still cool and a fine mist hovered over the vines as they walked to the house, straight through to the kitchen where she lit the stove with the sparker. He took in the new propane cylinder, then picked up and inspected an ancient but well-scrubbed saucepan on the stove.

"You've been busy," he said. There was admiration in his voice and she treasured it. She opened the small packets of coffee she'd taken from her hotel room into the two tin cups she'd found in the pantry. When the water boiled she put both cups on a tray and carried them out to the picnic table prouder than if she'd been serving tea in china cups at the Palace Hotel in San Francisco. The smell of the coffee mingled with the smell of the dew on the overgrown grass poking up around ancient stepping stones. Dario was watching her so intently she almost dropped the tray.

"It's just coffee," she said modestly. "Next time I'll make bread. Now that I have a working oven."

He sipped his coffee. "Not bad," he said with a smile that melted her heart. She smiled in return, proud of herself for achieving a way to heat water. The coffee was hot and strong and on top of the adrenaline pumping through her veins, she was ready for a full day's work.

Then there was his smile. Another stimulant. With just his smile she needed no coffee. Not to mention his company. He kept her entertained with stories of how he learnt to make wine and the times he had had to chase off the wild boars. But when he finally left she sat on an old wooden chair on the patio, suddenly as limp as a rag doll, exhausted and light-headed and more confused than ever. They kissed each other again— beautiful kisses that made her feel amazing—but what did it mean? Had they begun a relationship, an affair? She didn't ask when she'd see him again and he didn't say. She wished she didn't care so much.

Dario drove slowly down the road toward town. He'd done what he had to do, what anyone would do for a neighbor, he'd chased off the boars. But Isabel wasn't just any neighbor; she was like a magnet and it was hard to resist a magnetic force. He'd resisted for a few days, but he still hadn't been able to push her out of his mind. He'd finally given in and come here and now he knew he couldn't stay away.

It wasn't just the way she looked in a turquoise dress or in a nightgown or the fact that she changed a tire by herself. It wasn't just the way she followed him through the vines as he shot pellets at the boars instead of watching from the window like any other woman would do. It wasn't only her pride in making coffee in an old kitchen with nothing but a few packets. It was her determination in the face of obstacles and the fact that he could not let her face these obstacles alone. It was all of these things put together. And something more. Something he refused to analyze.

That night he was back at the Azienda, telling himself and her that the boars were likely to come again. It was true, they were determined and hungry beasts. He wasn't the only one who thought so, all the growers were on alert. It was only prudent to be prepared. This time he was so prepared that he brought steaks, potatoes and a bottle of Chianti.

"I owe you a dinner since you shared yours with me at the hotel," he explained. The smile she gave him made him regret the nights he'd stayed away. He could have been here with her, feeling the warm radiance of that smile.

They cooked outside at the fire pit. There was plenty of old firewood stacked in the barn. He was being a good neighbor. It was a tradition. In Sicily you don't let your neighbor go hungry.

They ate on the weathered oak picnic table behind the house. In the middle of the table was a pitcher with the pink fragrant Queen Isabella roses his sister had given her. How aptly named, he thought. Isabel was like a rose, so pink and lovely he wanted to inhale her fragrance.

They talked about the harvest and the grapes, then he asked about life in California. She told him San Francisco was full of fit, bright young people who enjoyed the outdoors, ate salads and fresh Dungeness crab out of the ocean.

"California sounds like paradise," he said. "What made you leave? I know, a miracle happened and you inherited a vineyard. But what really made you leave? Was it because of your boss? The one who lied to you?"

Isabel turned her wineglass around in her hand before she spoke.

"That's right. I was ready for a big change after I got fired for breaking the company rule, no inter-office dating."

"You were fired? I thought no one knew."

"I thought so, too."

"What happened to him?"

"Nothing at all. He's still there."

"But he broke the rule, too."

"I know what you're thinking. It's not fair. But if I have learned anything it is that life is not fair. Was it fair my parents died? Was it fair the foster families didn't want me? But my luck changed when my uncle left me this place. Was it fair he left it to me and didn't sell it to you? I don't know, but I'm not going to complain, not about anything." She folded her arms across her waist as if she was still protecting herself from any more hurt.

He leaned across the table to brush a tendril of red-gold hair from her cheek.

"I have no excuse for what happened between me and him. After years of telling myself not to believe, not to trust anyone but myself, I knew I was on my own and always would be. Then I forgot it all and made a huge mistake. I thought I'd never get over it."

"But you did," he insisted. "You're back on your feet. You've got gumption and drive and you're the hardest worker I've ever seen." *And you're beautiful, bright and courageous.*

She blushed at the compliment, her cheeks turning pink. She was the most amazing combination of modesty and confidence. The thought of anyone hurting her filled him with rage.

"Thanks to my uncle and this vineyard, which gave me something to do. A reason to try. A new place, a new job. Everything I needed but didn't know it. That's the miracle I was telling you about. When I got the letter from the lawyer I thought it was a message from heaven. It was my ticket to a new life, a life I could live without help from anyone." She stopped and looked at him. "Except you. I don't know what I would do without you to help me."

He wanted to take her in his arms and tell her he'd always help her, that she'd never be alone again. But he couldn't say that. He couldn't make any such promises, not to her, not to anyone.

"Anyone would have done it. I just happened to be around." As if he would be there with dinner if it had been someone else. She'd broken through his reserve the way no one else could have. "Next thing, you should learn Italian," he said.

"I know. Every day I realize how difficult life is when you don't speak the language. I can't even read the newspaper."

In a moment she was back with the local newspaper. He opened it up and together they translated an article. He couldn't help laughing at her pronunciation of certain words in Italian. He was afraid he'd hurt her feelings, but she laughed with him. What a woman. What a remarkable woman. She seemed to be without an ego. Yes, he knew she was wounded and vulnerable, but tonight she seemed happy and relaxed and so sexy with her tousled hair and her sunburned face. Keep it neighborly, he told himself. Unless you can be sure she's ready for more.

"I think you're ready for advanced Italian tomorrow," he said.

"I need advanced Italian, but first I need running water. I got motor oil and gasoline and diesel for the pump, but…" She trailed off.

"Let's have a look at it." He got up and stretched. It was a good excuse to stop staring at Isabel, watching her lips as she pronounced the words in Italian, knowing how her mouth felt pressed against his, knowing how she felt in his arms and how she smelled like wildflowers. Much safer for his state of mind to face off against an ancient pump and try to make it work than to imagine holding her in his arms all night.

Isabel went to get the motor oil she'd bought and her flashlight and met him at the old pumphouse behind the wine cellar. She felt guilty prevailing on him to help her after he'd brought the dinner. But sitting across the table from him, sharing food, could become a habit she shouldn't get used to. Hadn't she confessed how stupid she'd been to fall for the wrong man?

Dario kneeled next to the antique cast-iron engine. "I'm not sure this old relic will run again. Shine the light down here. Now we need the wrenches. They should be in the toolbox in the wine cellar."

When she returned with the toolbox he struggled with the rusty drain plug, but it appeared to be frozen from years of disuse. She sighed with despair. She had the oil, the wrench and the expert and still no luck.

"This could be trouble. If we can't change the oil, we can't run the pump."

"Never mind, I'll bathe in mineral water after all."

He looked up and grinned at her. A real grin. Instead of criticizing her for being extravagant he just smiled. Her heart drummed against her ribs. She'd rather have him smile like that than have all the running water in the world.

"Just joking," she said. "What can I do to help?"

"Sit down." He motioned for her to take a position on the dirt floor opposite him. "I'll push on the wrench from this side, you pull from the other. Okay, pull!"

Together Isabel pulled and Dario pushed, their hands squeezed together on the wrench. Dario's straining calf pressed against her thigh. But the plug didn't budge. They rested. They tried again. Isabel's hair was hanging in damp tendrils; her face was dripping with sweat. She had to do her part. They had to make it work. She had to have running water if she was going to live here.

This time she put all her energy into it, pulling as hard as she could. Suddenly the plug broke free. Dario's straining body lunged forward and he fell against Isabel, who was now spreadeagled on her back. His chest pressed against hers, his legs on top of hers. For a long moment he didn't move and she didn't speak. She couldn't catch her breath and she didn't know what she would say if she could.

"Are you hurt?" he asked, his voice low and as intimate as his position on top of her.

"No."

Instead of taking advantage of the situation, the way she wished he would, he got up, then extended his hand to help her up. "Very good job, *signorina*," he said, "you'd make an excellent plumber."

She nodded, too tired to speak. And just a little disappointed he hadn't kissed her again. But it wasn't over yet. Next they drained the old oil into an olive-oil can and put the fresh fuel Isabel had bought into the engine's tank.

"Now comes the moment of truth, when we find out if we can wake up this creature from its sleep." He wound the starter cord around the pulley. If Dario couldn't make it work, no one could. But after several more tries, Dario was panting and nothing was happening.

"Can I try?" she asked anxiously.

He wrapped the cord around the pulley and handed her the wooden handle on the end. Then he stood behind her and wrapped his warm hand around hers. "Pull gently but firmly. Like this." She sighed. Life didn't get much better than that. Working together, learning together, making something happen.

His hand tightened on hers and they pulled together. The flywheel slowly turned as the cord unwound. The engine gave a little cough.

"Did you hear that?" she asked, her heart pounding.

"I think she's got some life in her yet," he said and poured some gasoline into the carburetor. "Stand back," he ordered. Then with one powerful pull on the cord the engine roared to life. He gave Isabel a thumbs-up and she'd never been so proud of herself in her life.

They primed the pump and she could hear the beautiful sound of water gurgling in the pipes. On the roof, which they reached by a long wooden ladder, she could see the water was now filling the tank.

"I think you may be able to have a shower tonight," he said.

She definitely needed a shower after being caked with dirt and sweat. Just as soon as he left. But he didn't leave. He said he was afraid the boars would be back.

"It's the season, you know. You can't take a chance on losing your vines."

Before she could protest that there was nowhere for him to sleep, he said there was a room for the servants behind a door in the kitchen she'd never opened. Inside was a bed and Dario said he'd be fine staying there.

By that time Isabel didn't have the energy to argue, and

why should she tell the man who had provided her with food and water to leave when she didn't want him to? Fortunately she'd bought extra sheets, a pillow and blankets, almost as if she knew something like this would happen. And she did feel safer having him there. Not only safer but happier.

He promised to hook up a tankless flash hot water for her the next day, but she thought a cold shower would feel wonderful. And it did. From the top of the stairs, she called to him.

"It's your turn," she said, wrapped in a towel.

He stood at the foot of the stairs and looked up at her. His face, only half-lit by the gas lantern, was all sharp lines and deep hollows. She sucked in a deep breath. There was a long silence. Their eyes locked and held. She told herself to move, to go to her room, but her feet wouldn't obey. Her skin tingled from the cold shower but his smoldering gaze made her feel as if she was burning up.

Was he thinking about how few steps stood between the two of them? Was he thinking of how few seconds it would take for her to walk down and throw herself into his arms? Or for him to climb up the steps and wrap his arms around her? She knew what it would feel like. Like heaven. But heaven was not what was in store for her. She knew it. She'd tried to find it before but it was always outside her grasp.

She had a house and a new life—more than she'd expected. She wouldn't wish for more. Her job was to stand on her own two feet. Nothing wrong with accepting help, but never should she count on it. Nothing wrong with a few kisses. As long as that's all it was. She was proud of her self-control.

Finally she relaxed her shoulders, then she sighed and turned and went to her bedroom with the hole in the roof and stared at the stars while he showered. She tried to think about the Milky Way and the constellations, but instead she thought about how he must look with the water coursing over his body, the drops catching in the hair on his chest. No wonder she couldn't sleep.

Later, Dario lay in the bed in the old servants' quarters on top of a blanket he kept in his car. The window was wide open and he didn't need any cover. He wanted to feel the breeze on his bare body and think about Isabel upstairs. Was she having as much trouble sleeping as he was? Was she thinking what he was thinking? Why hold back when they were attracted to each other? Why stop when they were in the prime of life with normal passions kept buried too long?

They were both mature adults with realistic expectations, that is to say, none at all. They were sleeping under the same roof, working toward the same goal—producing fine wine— his family liked her and she continued to amaze and surprise him. After she'd been betrayed by the married man, she'd suffered, but then she'd rebounded remarkably. It was good to know she wasn't interested in a long-term relationship any more than he was.

Too restless to stay in bed, he pulled on his jeans and went to the kitchen where he found a bottle of cold sparkling water. When he heard footsteps on the stairs he set the bottle down and leaned back against the counter. Had she heard him come into the kitchen?

It was the second time he'd seen Isabel in her sheer night-gown, so transparent he could see her breasts, her stomach, and her long legs in the bright moonlight that shone through the window. He grabbed the back of a chair to keep his balance. How was a man supposed to resist this kind of temp-tation? She stood in the doorway blinking in surprise. Every fiber of his being called out to her, but his voice was silent— until he finally said, "You can't sleep either?"

"Just thirsty," she said in a half whisper, half sigh.

He held out his bottle. She took it.

"What about you? That bed must be hard as cement."

"It's not the bed. It's you. I was thinking about you." He paused. "You're good for me. You've made me break out of the shell I was in."

"What did Magdalena do to you?" she asked softly.

He sucked in a deep breath. She'd told him about her ex, and he'd already told her about Magdalena, but it was time he came completely clean about what had happened. He pulled out a chair and straddled it. She sat across the table from him, her chin propped in her hand. Her hair was in a tangle around her face. She smelled like fine-milled soap and she looked as though she'd just stepped out of his dream.

"I told you she and I went off together when she was crowned Miss Sicily and I neglected the vineyards. That was bad enough. I justified it by thinking we would eventually get married and settle down here at Encanto on the family estate. Then I'd have no more distractions. Magdalena's reign as Miss Sicily would be over and she'd be as happy as I was to stay home.

"But that was not the future Magdalena wanted. To her, Sicily was the last outpost of civilization. She wanted out of the island altogether, but she didn't tell me or anyone that or she'd lose her title. So she finished out the year and then ran off with my cousin Georgio from Milan. He's a very well-to-do businessman who came to our engagement party and made a pass at her without my knowing. She saw he was her ticket out of here and she took it. I was blindsided. Completely fooled. I had no idea." He buried his head in his hands. "Sometimes it still feels like it happened yesterday," he said.

"I'm sorry," she said. "I think I know how you must have felt."

He raised his head. He stared off into space. "Like the

volcano had erupted and buried me in hot ashes. Like all the color had been drained from the world. Everything was in black and white. Mostly black. Some gray. I walked around, I went to work in the fields, I managed the harvest, but at the end of each day I had no idea how I'd gotten through it. My mind was blank. It was the only way I knew to survive. I felt nothing, not the heat or the cold or the rain. I was numb. You could have done open-heart surgery on me without an anesthetic." He gave a hollow laugh. "Maybe that's what happened. They opened me up, looked at my heart and saw it was broken, cracked in half. They shook their heads and said, 'No chance of repair.'"

"Oh, Dario," she said, reaching for his hand. There was sympathy and understanding in her eyes, but no pity. If anyone understood it would be Isabel and he was grateful.

He stared off into space. "I never told anyone what I was going through, but the family guessed, which is why they hold such a grudge against Magdalena." He rubbed his chin. "I did survive, as you see. Color came back to the fields and the vines. The sky was blue again. The sun rose and set a few hundred times and I was an older, wiser man, I hope. So don't feel sorry for me."

She shook her head.

They sat there for a few minutes, then she touched his cheek, as soft as a feather, and she stood and reached for his hand. He didn't have to ask what it meant. The answer was in her face, in the way she clasped his hand. She wanted him as much as he wanted her. They both knew what would happen next as they walked up the narrow stairway to the bedroom and the narrow bed meant for one. Meant for one, but just right for two people who'd been waiting for this moment since the first time they'd met on that dusty road.

As the stars faded and the sky grew light, they lay together, wedged at the hip, legs entwined, arms flung around each other. Lying there, happier than she ever remembered, with Dario's face half buried in the pillow, Isabel relived the night spent making glorious, passionate love with Dario under the stars, the most amazing night she'd ever had. She said a prayer to the heavens and whatever gods were listening—*Please, please don't let me fall in love with him.*

But it was too late.

CHAPTER NINE

THE NEXT DAY was Saturday. Isabel didn't expect her workers but she heard a truck in her driveway in the morning. She looked at Dario, sleepy-eyed, his hair falling across his forehead. He raised his head, propped himself on his elbow and kissed her. If she'd thought last night was a dream, she knew now it was real. He was real and she was ecstatic. But a little worried too. What did it mean? What happened next?

"The bed's a little small," she said.

He grinned at her and her heart beat to a crazy rhythm. "Seemed just right to me," he said. "Although you're welcome to try mine the next time."

So there would be a next time. She returned his smile, then she remembered.

"Someone's here," she whispered as if afraid someone would hear and someone would know. A hangover from the old days, she knew, when an affair must be kept secret from the world. Some day she'd get over it, but not now. Not yet.

She jumped out of bed, surprised she'd slept at all, let alone so late. She felt his eyes on her as she stood naked in the small room and her sensitive skin burned. She dressed quickly in a pair of shorts and an old T-shirt.

"I'll go see who it is."

When she went to the front door she saw his sister Lucia standing on the steps with a basket in her hands. "I heard you'd checked out of the hotel and I was afraid you didn't have any food."

Isabel felt a moment of panic. Would she find out her brother was here? What would she think? More importantly what would *he* think if the word spread he was spending the night? "How nice. Thank you." She should invite her in, but if she ran into Dario, it could cause problems.

Lucia turned to look down the driveway. "That looks like Dario's car down there."

"Uh, yes, you see, he was afraid there'd be boars in the vineyards so he came by…" Her mind was racing so fast trying to come up with a plausible explanation, that she stumbled and her mind went blank.

"You don't have to explain to me," Lucia said with a small knowing smile on her lips. "I'll be off now, but I wanted to say I've spoken to the priest and he's free on a Saturday to do the Blessing if that's okay with you. He's also available for other ceremonies…like a wedding," she added with a gleam in her eye.

Isabel hoped Dario didn't hear her say that. Surely Lucia knew he'd never commit to another relationship. Neither would Isabel. And yet, despite the brick wall she'd so carefully built around her heart, she had a sudden vision of herself walking through the vineyard in a long white dress. She closed her eyes and forced herself to be strong. No wedding dreams, no letting her imagination run away with her. That was a sure way of getting caught in a melt-down she'd never recover from.

"Thank you. That should be fine," she told Lucia. "The Blessing I mean," she added hastily.

Lucia's gaze drifted to somewhere over Isabel's shoulder.

"Lucia, what are you doing here?" Dario asked. Isabel whirled around. Just as Lucia was about to leave, he had to appear. But he didn't sound angry at being caught in a compromising position, just surprised. Just one glance at his bare chest, his low-slung jeans and his hair standing on end made Isabel's heart leap and told her as well as his sister that he'd just gotten up and that he'd definitely, without question, spent the night with her. He didn't seem to care what anyone thought. What a change from her last affair, where the anxiety of being caught had left Isabel with a nagging pain in her chest.

"Lucia's brought us some food," Isabel said brightly. All she could think was that he looked so sexy with his eyes still filled with sleep that her pulse was racing. She had an urge to run her hand around the outline of his rough jaw. She wanted to press her cheek against his bronzed chest and listen to his heart to see if it was beating as fast as hers. Instead she clenched her hands into fists and told herself to be strong.

"Thanks," Dario said casually to his sister.

Feeling as relaxed as he seemed to be, Isabel said to Lucia, "Won't you come in for some coffee?"

Lucia said she had to go home, then she headed back down the driveway. Before she got into her car, she turned to look at them for a long moment. Isabel waved.

"I don't know what she must think," she said to Dario, still slightly anxious.

"She thinks we're having an affair."

"Are we?" Waiting for his answer, her heart hammered so loudly she was afraid Lucia could hear it from where she stood.

"Aren't we?" he answered with a devastating smile that warmed her heart and curled her bare toes.

Isabel breathed a sigh of relief. The contrast between him and Neil, her one-time fiancé, was startling in every way. Her ex-boss had worried constantly about being found out. When they had been found out, it was she who'd suffered, not him.

He pulled her tightly against him and kissed her throat, her chin, her eyelids and finally her mouth.

"Why not have an affair?" he asked when he let her go at last. "We get along well, if last night was any indication."

She blushed. Yes they got along extremely well.

"We're both free of obligations," he continued.

"As long as we both know we can come and go at will. That is, no strings," she said firmly. "No promises. No commitment." She said these things for herself to hear as well as for him. The rules had to be agreed on, whether she liked them or not.

He nodded solemnly, put his arm around her and they went inside.

She asked herself how could anything that felt this good be bad? As long as no one got hurt, and Isabel knew better than to let herself get hurt. She needed his help on the vineyard. He wanted to help her. Instead of fighting for the property, they were both working toward one goal—to turn the grapes into fine wine. It was as simple as that.

After eating a half dozen delicious *cornetti*, the crescent-shaped local pastries Lucia had brought, and drinking more coffee, Dario walked out to the vineyard. The sun was shining on a run-down house and rows of neglected vines, and the world had never looked so good to him. Isabel was beautiful, wonderful, kind and generous, and for now she was all his. Before he let himself wallow in contentment, he saw with alarm that there was water gushing up from the ancient water pipe buried under the ground. Just when he'd repaired the pump, gotten water into the house and filled the tank on top of the roof, now this. He turned off the water at the pumphouse, got a shovel from the shed and dug down to expose a length of pipe. But he couldn't tell where the break was.

"The water pipe's broken," he called to Isabel. She came running from the house. "I need you."

"What happened?" she asked breathlessly.

"The pipe's old, it sprang a leak so the water's not getting to the vines. We'll have to replace it." Even in the heat of the battle with the leaky pipe, he realized he'd said *we* when he meant *you*. After all, it was her pipe.

"You stay here. I'll turn the water back on and you tell me where it's coming from."

She nodded. A few minutes later he heard her shriek. He ran back and found her drenched in water from the spray.

"Good, you found it," he said, his gaze riveted to her shirt plastered to her breasts and her shorts clinging to her hips.

She looked so surprised with her hair dripping down her face and her shirt and shorts soaked to her body, he burst out laughing despite the situation.

She laughed too and they stood looking at each other, water gushing from the pipe, until the laughter died and she was in his arms again, where she belonged, her breasts pressed against his chest, his shirt wet. He knew right away he was ready to go back up to the bedroom and continue where they'd left off. In fact, they might still be there if his sister hadn't appeared.

It was a good thing they had an agreement. Nothing serious. He'd been hurt, so had she. This affair of theirs was part of the healing process, and he'd never felt so happy as when he had Isabel in his arms. Still, there was good reason not to lose their heads. He'd never take a chance on love again and she wouldn't either. He'd learned the hard way. Besides, there was work to be done here. "I'd better get this thing repaired," he said abruptly.

"Need my help?" she asked, stepping backwards.

He shook his head. "You go change." Because if she didn't change into dry clothes, and he couldn't stop holding her and planning about how he'd like to take her clothes off and make love all afternoon, then he'd better get out of here. And that was something he didn't want to do.

After the pipe repair, Dario went up to the roof to get his mind back to work, while Isabel whitewashed the cellar. When she started painting the front of the house, he held the ladder for her.

"You're brave," he noted. "The ladder hasn't been used for years."

"I'm only brave when there are no boars around," she said from her perch under the shingles of the roof.

That night they searched the basket Lucia brought and found homemade pasta, pesto sauce, fresh tomatoes, Parmesan cheese and sausage his grandfather had made. But first they each had a refreshing shower, now available with either hot or cold running water. He thought it best to wait outside the house until she had finished showering. Then he changed his mind. The sound of running water and the picture of her standing naked under the shower had a profound effect on him. Why wait for her to finish her shower when it would save water if they showered together? As he bounded up the stairs, he wondered where Dario the workaholic had gone? He'd changed since she arrived. That much he knew.

It bothered him to remember that the last time he'd changed was when he'd followed Magdalena from one end of the island to the other allowing his vineyards to go to ruins. But this was different. He wasn't neglecting anything. As long as he was in control of the situation, no worry. He knocked on the bathroom door, tossed his clothes on the floor and joined her in the shower.

"It's more than I expected," she said when they came downstairs after the shower. Dario's hair was still wet, his body still responding to hers in the most primitive way. She sat outside while she dried her hair in the late-afternoon sun. "Cold water would have made me happy, but make that hot water and you add it up to pure bliss."

Bliss is what she radiated. Bliss is what he felt too. Dario couldn't take his eyes from her face and the sight of her copper-colored hair gleaming in the sun. He hadn't smiled much for at least a year. But now, every day and every hour, something Isabel said or did made his mouth curve upward.

She was so warm, so generous, that he felt like a new person in a new world, a world he was getting used to. He already knew she was gutsy, dedicated, and determined to get the house in order as well as supervise the harvest. She was also so much fun to be with he sometimes stopped working just to watch her standing on the top of the ladder, a smudge of paint on her nose, and he'd catch himself staring at her wondering how long this could last.

Days went by. Long sunny days followed by balmy starlit nights together in her narrow bed. She painted the kitchen and made curtains for the bedroom. He worked on his own harvest in the morning, but joined her every day for a long lunch. "It's a Sicilian tradition," he explained. It was also a Sicilian tradition to make love in the afternoon on long summer days. Then back to work.

In the evening he'd return for dinner laden with supplies and they cooked together, ate together, talked together, laughed and kissed and fell into bed at night, tired, but never too tired to take their relationship to a new level of intimacy. As long as they both knew the rules.

Sometimes, even when Dario wasn't helping her out at the

Azienda, he felt as if he was standing on the top of a ladder. Not only on top of the ladder, but on top of the world. He had no idea how long his mood would last. One week passed, then two weeks and he was still on top of the world. But the last time he'd been this close to a woman their happy affair had come crashing down around him. The warning voice inside his head got more muted each day. He knew it wouldn't happen again because he would never let himself go the way he had. He was holding back, keeping his heart and soul locked away.

Of course, Isabel was a different kind of woman than Magdalena and he was a different man than he was then. He was a man with defenses firmly in place around his heart. If he still had a heart, which he sometimes doubted, it had hardened into Sicilian granite. Which wasn't a bad thing under the circumstances.

But waking up each morning in bed with Isabel was something else. He liked seeing her every morning, her glorious red hair tousled, her eyes sleepy. He liked seeing her every night, her hair damp from the shower, and just before she fell asleep she murmured *buona notte* to him. It seemed natural. It seemed right.

The approval of his family when they learned he was spending even more time at the Azienda with Isabel was a nice change from their worried frowns and negative remarks during the Magdalena era.

But still, he knew this affair wouldn't last. They had a goal—to prepare the place for the Blessing of the Grapes. After that something would change. Either he'd go back to his house full time or... By then she'd have power and water and a telephone and she wouldn't need him to stay there anymore. She wouldn't need him at all. That was a good thing. At least he'd thought so until today, over two weeks since the first night he'd spent there. Now he wondered how much he would miss not being needed, miss being a part of her daily life.

Sitting at the picnic table after dinner when the air was cool, drinking wine and talking or just sitting there as night fell and the breeze came up made him feel that life couldn't get much better than this. Isabel had cooked the whole dinner after a hard day of work grouting the bathroom floor because he was late.

"Tomorrow night I'm taking you to the hotel for dinner," he said. "For a change. You've been working so hard here, you need a break."

She looked up, her eyes wide, her cheeks flushed in the light from the gas lantern hanging from a branch of the sycamore tree.

"You don't have to do that," she said.

"But I want to show you off. You'll wear your blue dress and I'll even wear a clean shirt. I want everyone to see me having dinner with the beautiful American winemaker."

CHAPTER TEN

THE NEXT NIGHT Isabel showered and scrubbed the paint off her fingers before putting on her one and only dress. She loved cooking with Dario and for Dario in her own rustic kitchen every night, but when he'd invited her to dinner at the hotel, she'd had to stop abruptly and think. This was a date. They were having an affair, but this was their first date. She hadn't had a real date for years. Certainly not with Neil.

Her mind was still reeling. He wanted to show her off. He wanted people to see them together. It was all so new, so amazingly different from her last affair. It made her feel wanted and desired…but not loved. If he loved her she'd know it. But he didn't. His words echoed in her brain—*it won't happen again.* She understood that. He'd loved Magdalena, but he'd never love again. She felt the same. It didn't matter. Love was greatly oversold.

When she came downstairs he turned to look at her. His mouth fell open. He looked as stunned as if he'd never seen her before, when he'd seen her every day of the past fourteen.

"What's wrong?" she asked, nervously adjusting the spaghetti strap of her dress. She hadn't worn it since that night at his house. She hadn't been back there since.

"You look beautiful," he said soberly.

Then it was her turn to stare. He was so gorgeous in a white shirt that contrasted with his dark hair and showed off his tan that she felt as though she'd never seen him before.

The wind whipped her hair against her cheek as they drove down the hill to the hotel. He took his eyes off the road from time to time to look at her and she felt the heat from his gaze.

They had drinks in the bar. Dario ordered Bellinis for them, ripe white peaches mixed with champagne, and he introduced her to several of his friends. They made small talk about wine and grapes until they went into the dining room.

"So much has happened since I left this hotel," she said looking around at the familiar white tablecloths and the flowers on every table. "I hardly feel like the same person who bumbled her way to the Azienda. I have you to thank for taking me there and making me feel at home."

He shook his head. "You did it on your own. You wouldn't let anyone or anything stand in your way. Anyone else would have turned around and gone home after one look at the Azienda. Not you." He sent her a dazzling smile with no hint of regret in it, at least that's what she wanted to think.

Before they ordered, a bottle of dry sparkling white wine was brought to the table and a waiter in a black vest poured two glasses.

"To the future," Dario said, tapping his glass against hers. "But first we have to bury the past. I've told you more than you want to know about my past and Magdalena, but you haven't told me how you got fired."

She took a sip of wine then set her glass down. "I'd rather not talk about it. I'd rather forget it."

"You can't forget something until it's gone, dead and buried and out of sight." He paused. "Believe me, I know. Some other time then," he said with a shrug.

She knew it was time to come clean with the whole story, no matter how painful. It was only fair. He'd told her about Magdalena and now it was her turn. But when the *calamare fritti* came with a delicious spicy sauce she didn't want to spoil the mood or the dinner so she changed the subject. The salad was her favorite, made of spinach with ribbons of *pancetta* and sprinkled with chunks of creamy gorgonzola cheese. It was so delicious and he was being so entertaining and making her smile with stories of his childhood, she couldn't change the subject and start talking about her disastrous affair. Especially when the main course arrived— pasta with smoked salmon in a brandy cream sauce. She sighed with contentment as she spooned the last drop of sauce from her plate.

"The last time I ate dinner here was the night I moved to the Azienda," she said. "It was early and I was the only one in the dining room." What a difference. Tonight she was eating with the best-looking, most desirable man in Sicily. Tonight the place was full of couples and families, happily talking, drinking and eating. Not a single person was alone. It was almost a crime in Sicily to eat alone. Food was for sharing. Life was for sharing. How far she'd come in just a few weeks. How much farther would she go?

After coffee they strolled out to his car. She still hadn't answered his questions. She didn't know how to start. So she waited until they got back to the Azienda and were sitting on the newly painted front veranda, on a large swing he'd brought her as a housewarming present.

They sat in companionable silence for a long time swinging back and forth while the stars glittered in the sky above them. *Tell him, tell him,* said the voice inside her head. *It's not going to get any easier.*

"All right," she said at last, unable to prolong the silence any more. "You asked me how I got fired. His wife found out. I don't know how. But one day she burst into his office while I was there. We weren't doing anything, just talking. But she was furious. She screamed at me, called me names. I tried to tell her I was as shocked as she was, I'd had no idea that Neil was married. The next day I had fifteen minutes to clear my desk and leave the building. I was humiliated, and I was angry. *Why me,* I thought. Especially when I learned he hadn't been fired, he hadn't even been punished. In fact, he got promoted."

The memory of the shame and humiliation caused all the air in her lungs to leave. She took a deep breath. "The next week I dressed in a suit and went to see him to get a recommendation I knew I'd need if I ever applied for a job again. I thought it was the least he could do."

She hated talking about it. And yet, Dario was right. It was time to bury the past. If she couldn't tell Dario, then she couldn't tell anyone.

"He said he couldn't do it. He treated me as if *I'd* seduced *him*. As if it was all my fault. He said I deserved to be fired. I felt so sick I rushed out to the street. I started to believe he was right, that somehow I deserved what had happened to me. That was still my mood when I got the letter from the lawyer. After job-hunting for months, avoiding friends and sinking deeper and deeper into depression, I got the letter. I was an heiress. I had someplace to go and something to do. I studied Italian, I read up on winemaking. I had a goal, a purpose to my life."

He put his arm around her shoulders and held her tightly against him, her head on his shoulder. She could have stayed there forever.

"You wonder how I could ever have loved somebody like that," she said. "You have to realize that he not only told me I was a brilliant designer, he said I was beautiful and he loved me."

She leaned back, still feeling the support of Dario's arm around her. "No one had ever treated me that way before. No one had loved me before. One thing I'd learned long ago and that was not to cry. When it all fell apart, the day his wife found out and confronted us, I didn't cry. Because, if you cry, people will mock you or feel sorry for you. I'm not sure what is worst."

"So you came to Sicily."

"Thanks to my uncle."

"But it still hurts." It wasn't a question. It was as if he knew.

She turned her head to look up at him. His eyes were deep pools of understanding. "Yes. No. Not as much." *Not since you came into my life.* "I have other things to think about now. The grapes, the harvest, the Blessing, the house." *And you.*

And then she broke the one rule she'd always lived by. She started to cry. After all these years and all the rejections, all the hurt feelings, all the insults and all the sleepless nights she'd kept the tears from flowing. Maybe it was the night or Dario or the memories she'd uncovered. Whatever it was, once she started she couldn't stop. A lifetime of tears poured from her eyes onto his shoulder, onto his chest, dampening his beautiful clean white shirt.

"Tesoro don' grido di t…" he said. She didn't understand the words, but they made her feel better anyway. After an eternity, when she was finally cried out, she lay exhausted with her head in his lap looking up at the stars. And saying to herself the same prayer she said every night. *Please God, don't let me fall in love again.*

The Saturday of the Blessing was a brilliant, hot sunny day, like all the others. The early-morning mist that hung over the vines had disappeared by eight in the morning when the workers arrived with huge steel drums to fill with charcoal and cook the meat over a makeshift grill. Isabel stood at the edge of the vineyard, looking out at the fields below, her heart pounding with anticipation when Dario came up behind her and put his arms around her.

"Excited?" he said.

"And a little worried. What if the priest forgets to come? What if the wine from the cellar isn't good enough? What if I didn't order enough food." *What if I've fallen in love with you and you don't love me back?* It was her worst fear and her current nightmare. After two glorious weeks together—working together, eating together and sleeping together and getting things ready for the Blessing—today was the pinnacle. It would be a turning point. They'd either go forward or backward. She studied Dario's face for a clue to how he felt. At the end of the day, would he take his clothes and his tools and go home? Or would he tell her the words she wanted to hear. *I love you Isabel. I want to spend my life with you. Not just two weeks, but forever.*

He turned her around in his arms and pressed his finger against her lips.

"It's going to be a perfect day," he said. "You'll see. It's not the end, it's just the beginning."

She nodded. If only he meant that the way she wanted him to mean it. She had high hopes for the day, a beautiful ceremony, delicious food and wonderful new friends to share it with. It should be enough, but she wanted more. She wanted Dario.

What was wrong with her? Why couldn't she be happy with what she had? A house and a working vineyard. She didn't want to admit it, but she knew she'd made a terrible mistake. She'd fallen in love with Dario. When did it happen?

The night he came to shoot the boars? The night he took her to his house and kissed her? Or was it that first day when she saw him standing by the side of the road?

Whenever it was, she'd have to get over it. Unless he felt the same. Today she'd tell him how she felt. How else would she know if he loved her too? If he didn't, why had he moved into her house, why had he fed her, helped her, fixed her roof, repaired her water heater? Held her, kissed her, made love to her and let the world see they were a couple?

If he didn't love her, would she continue her life without him? She couldn't go on seeing him day and night like this if there was no future for them. If he didn't love her now he never would. It was time to find out the truth before it was too late for her to recuperate.

People started arriving mid morning, wearing their Sunday best, all Dario's relatives, including his grandfather in a wheelchair. They assembled in the meadow. The priest was there in his flowing robe. Dario was wearing a suit and Isabel almost fainted when she saw how gorgeous he looked in the white shirt and contrasting dark jacket and tie. His face was sun-browned and his eyes bluer than ever.

"You look beautiful," he said to her, his gaze lingering on the bodice of her turquoise dress, the same dress she'd worn at his house, the same dress she'd worn the night she'd finally let down her defenses and told him what had happened to her. She managed a little smile, too nervous and excited to compliment him in return. Or to tell him she loved him. Or ask if he loved her.

The tantalizing smell of pork roasting on a spit blended with the warm grass, the sweet smell of crushed grapes and the summer sunshine. The priest took his place at the edge of the clearing facing the crowd.

"God watereth the hills from above: the earth is filled with the fruit of thy works. He bringeth forth grass for the cattle, and green herb for the service of man: that he may bring food out of the earth; and wine that maketh glad the heart of man. Psalms 104: 13-14." When he blessed a basket of Amarado grapes Isabel felt a rush of emotion so strong she almost fainted. It was all so beautiful. So bittersweet. The beginning of her life as a winemaker on her own and the end of being Dario's protégée, always able to count on him being around. Unless...unless...

After the short service, Isabel saw Dario deep in conversation with his brother, Cosmo, and two sisters. He was frowning. His sister had her hand on his shoulder. She felt a slight shiver of fear go up her spine. Something had happened. Something was wrong.

She kissed the guests on both cheeks, she thanked them all for coming, she served the food and all the while she kept Dario and his family in view, wondering and worrying.

Finally he broke away from his relatives and joined her at the edge of the clearing.

"I have to leave," he said. "There's a problem. The dock workers in Palermo are on strike and our wine has been sitting on the dock for two weeks. It's my fault. I've been out of touch. The family didn't want to bother me while I was with you, they thought they could handle it." He paused. "They can't."

Isabel felt cold all over despite the heat from the noonday sun. She had a terrible feeling that history was repeating itself. Once again Dario had been distracted from his work by a woman. Her. And he felt guilty, maybe he even resented her for keeping him here helping her when he should have been paying attention to Montessori wine instead of her.

"I'm heading for Palermo now, today." He glanced around

at the party in full swing, the friends and neighbors eating and drinking together, but she wondered if he even noticed them with his mind on his problem.

"Dario, I'll miss you," she said softly. Now was not the time to tell him she loved him. Maybe after he got back.

"I'll be back in a week or two if all goes well. But you'll be fine without me," he said. "You're on your way. The house is livable and the grapes are ripe. You'll have a great harvest. You're strong. You're capable."

I may be capable, but I need you every day in every way, she thought, her heart pounding. What he was really saying was good-bye. Things would never be the same. He left without kissing her good-bye. His mind was hundreds of miles away. While she had been falling in love he had been just helping a neighbor. The truth hit her like a barrel of aged wine. Once again she'd fooled herself into thinking the man she loved loved her in return.

When everyone left, and the sun was setting over the hills in the distance, silence descended on the Azienda. Isabel looked around from the house to the vines. She sat down on a wooden chair at the edge of the vineyard, suddenly so tired and weak she felt as if she'd just run a marathon instead of hosting a party.

For the first time in two weeks, she was alone. She'd been spoiled. She'd let herself get used to having Dario there every night and every morning. Worst of all, she'd let herself fall in love with him. Finally she stood and went into her house, her cold, empty, lonely house.

During the next week Isabel took her grapes to be crushed. She continued to paint and plaster. She managed to buy food for herself, but she didn't feel like eating it. She went to bed every night and lay tossing and turning and thinking about how stupid she'd been until it got light. Life on the Azienda was no longer beautiful. It was flat and uninteresting without Dario. She gave herself stern warnings about standing strong, but she buried her head in her pillow and tuned them out.

Another week went by during which she talked to no one but her workers, and their conversation was limited by her lack of Italian. She was anxious to know how Dario was doing in Palermo, but she had no way to find out except by calling him on his cell phone, and she couldn't do that. She had her pride, after all.

If he wanted to get in touch with her, he knew where to find her. One day she ran into Lucia at the town square. Dario's sister greeted her warmly.

"How's Dario doing?" Isabel asked, swallowing what little pride she had left.

"Still in Palermo. The problems are more serious than we thought. He's working night and day to negotiate a new contract with the workers' union. Who knows how long it will take? In the meantime Cosmo is taking over some of his work here. It's good for him. Dario was always the big brother. Always in charge. Cosmo never had a chance to show what he can do. Now's his chance."

Isabel felt sick. He'd updated his family, but hadn't called her.

"Are you all right?" Lucia asked. "You look a little pale."

Isabel managed a smile. "I'm fine."

Lucia looked at her and Isabel was afraid she could guess that she'd been suffering. "You know I was hoping you and Dario…"

"We were just friends, that's all," Isabel assured her.

"It's too bad," Lucia said softly. "You were good for him. I don't understand what happened."

Isabel understood perfectly. He'd made the same mistake

with her that he had with Magdalena except that he'd been in love with Magdalena. He was once again making up for his lack of attention to work by burying himself in it. This time for good. No one can recover from two mistakes in a row. Not Dario and not her either. It was time to do something different. She couldn't continue to live and work where Dario's face and his voice and his hands infused in every square inch of the house and land. Everywhere she looked she saw his smile, heard his voice and listened for his car. Every surface she touched, she felt him. It was an illusion. He wasn't there and he would never be there again, not the way she wanted him to be. She had to pull herself together and stop thinking about him night and day. She had to make decisions based on what was best for her and her state of mind. Hard decisions.

Dario was exhausted. He'd been working nonstop since he got to Palermo. He'd been up for the last twenty-four hours haggling over details with the union organizers. The days had all blended together since he'd left home. Home. Where was home? When he thought about it, the Azienda came into his mind. The Azienda and Isabel.

He tried not to think about her, but the sound of her voice, the look on her face before she woke up in the morning, the smell of fresh paint on her house, the taste of the coffee she made for him in the morning haunted him day and night. He couldn't shake the image of how she had looked when he'd said he was leaving. She'd tried to smile, but her lips had trembled. He'd thought he had no choice but to go. His mind was already there, settling the dispute. Fixing the problem by himself the way he always did.

He'd thought no one could handle the situation but him, but

his brother-in-law had arrived the night before with new energy and fresh ideas, so maybe he was wrong. He'd thought no one could manage the harvest without him, but Cosmo seemed to be doing fine. Maybe his family was right. He was a control freak who couldn't let go. But he couldn't do everything by himself. It was time to go home. He knew where home was. It was the Azienda. It was wherever Isabel was. He needed her. Without her he could never be whole. Never be happy.

Finally the answer came to Isabel. She had to leave. But how could she when she loved the Azienda, every crack in the foundation, every spiderweb, every dripping faucet. With all its flaws, it was the only home she'd ever had. Still, the pain was unbearable. The loneliness worse than ever. She'd been alone before, but that was before she met Dario. That was before she'd shared this house and her bed and her life with him. She could be alone again, but not here. He'd made it impossible for her to stay.

She went to Dario's house and looked in the window. She saw the stone fireplace and the matching leather chairs and the pile of papers untouched on his desk. She remembered how she'd felt the night he'd brought her here to see his grandfather's paintings and had kissed her for the first time.

There was no music playing today. The windows were closed. She slid the note she'd written under his front door. When he walked in it would be the first thing he'd see. She was glad he wasn't there. If he were, he'd try to convince her to stay. He'd give her all the reasons why she should stay, except for the one she wanted to hear. She leaned against his front door, her head pressed against the hard wood panel. *What am I doing?* She asked herself. *I can't leave.* She had to retrieve the note. But she couldn't reach it. She'd write another one, she'd say—*Disregard the previous note. I'm not leaving after all. It's nothing personal. Nothing to do with you. I just can't leave a house I've spent so much time and energy on.*

Then she reminded herself he hadn't called her since he'd left. He didn't miss her. He didn't love her. It was obvious. The brusque way he'd left her the day of the Blessing was like a fresh wound in her heart. He didn't seem at all sorry he had to go. He appeared almost eager for a new challenge. Why had she not realized what it meant? Once again she'd fallen in love by herself. It was time to go or to consign herself to suffering even more than she was now. Or should she wait and tell him in person? She went to her car and sat there for an hour, torn between going and staying.

Dario returned from Palermo that night. He had to see Isabel. He had to see her right now. He'd thought he didn't need her. He'd thought he'd lost his head again, along with his work ethic. Instead he'd found what was important. More important than the land or the harvest or anything. It was her. He went straight to the Azienda, but she wasn't there. The door was unlocked but the house was empty. Puzzled and confused, with a sense of dread gnawing at his gut, he went to his house.

When he saw her note lying on his floor he dumped his valise on the ground and sat down at his desk, his heart pounding, his vision blurred as he read her words.

"…can't stay here any longer…too difficult…I understand…Azienda all yours…" He crumpled the note in his hand and threw it across the room. What was wrong with her? Why did she leave? Was it because he'd gone to Palermo and she needed him? Why didn't she get in touch with him then? She'd never called him once while he was gone. The note was full of explanations, but none of them made any sense.

He was in a state of shock. He'd been working too hard, not eating enough, not sleeping enough, then driving here too fast, thinking about her too much.

He stared at the empty fireplace filled with cold ashes. He retrieved the note and smoothed the wrinkles in it with his palm. He walked outside and looked at the sky. The sun was still shining even though Isabel wasn't here. She'd gone back to California. But when and how?

He was filled with anger. Anger at her for leaving without telling him. Anger at himself because of all the things he'd never done. Never taken her to see the volcano. Never taken her to see the *cathedrale* at Monreale or to the opera to hear Puccini.

He stood for a long moment trying to get it through his head that she was gone. She wouldn't be there to share dinner cooked over an outdoor fire pit with him. She wouldn't be there to take a shower with him or put her arms around him to keep from rolling out of the narrow bed they'd shared.

He thought of the Azienda. Her touch and her smell were everywhere as if she'd just stepped out for a moment. Maybe she had. Maybe she'd just left. Maybe she wouldn't be able to get a ticket home. He could only hope. Missing her caused a dull ache in his heart, the heart he'd thought was encased in stone. So he ran back to his car and drove as fast as he could to the airport. He, the ultimate loner, the guy who lived alone was racing down the highway to try to persuade a woman to share her life with him. Forever.

Isabel was at the ticket counter where she'd been waiting for hours while the agent checked the flights to the U.S. again and again. Nothing. There was nothing today. Maybe *domani*... tomorrow?

She couldn't wait until tomorrow. She'd lose her nerve. She was already having second and third thoughts. If she didn't get on a plane now what would she do? Return to the Azienda? Go to a hotel? Buy a ticket to someplace else? No, no no. She paced the floor, bought a magazine and went to the airport *caffee* and ordered a cappuccino. If Dario were here he'd insist she get a gelato too. He wanted her to taste and experience everything Sicilian.

But he wasn't here. He was in Palermo working. That's where he wanted to be. The time he'd spent with her at the Azienda was just a blip on the screen of his life, only a short sequence that had been fun but that couldn't last. If it weren't for the family business emergency, it would have been something else. Yes, it was best she leave. If not today then tomorrow. And if not tomorrow...

"*Ciao, signorina*," he said, in a voice she recognized with a jolt.

She swiveled around on her chair and stared. There he was easing into a chair across the table as if this had all been planned. She gripped the spoon in her hand so tightly her knuckles turned white. She opened her mouth but no sound came out. He very casually ordered a coffee, so casually that she was convinced he'd seen her note and he had just come to say good-bye.

She braced herself against the back of the chair while her heart pounded and the whole room spun around. "What are you doing here?" she asked, her voice so strained she sounded like a rusty gate. It must be a dream. Dario at the airport.

He rested his elbows on the table and leaned toward her. He was so close she saw the fine lines at the corners of his eyes and the shadow of a beard that lined his jaw. He looked as if he hadn't slept for days. But he still looked amazing in his Italian jeans and his blue shirt. He was so close she felt her bones melt.

"I might ask you the same thing," he said. "What are you doing here?"

"I'm thinking of returning to California. But all the flights are full."

"Why?" he said, his blue eyes glittering like the sea on a stormy day.

"Why are they full?" she asked with a frown. "Maybe because it's Friday."

"Why are you leaving?" he asked, with an obvious effort to be patient with her.

"I wrote you a note," she explained

"I got your note. But I want to hear it from you. Straight from your mouth. I thought you liked it here."

"I did. I do. But I can't stay." She pressed her lips together and willed herself not to cry. She must stay calm and explain why she was leaving. If only she could make it clear in her own head. "I thought I could manage the Azienda by myself, but when you left I realized I couldn't."

"It's not like you to quit something you cared about so much."

"It wasn't an easy decision." That was the truth. In fact, she was still wavering.

"At least you could have waited until I got back to tell me in person. I thought I meant more to you than that." His mouth twisted into a frown. "You could have called me. I never heard from you."

"You didn't call *me*. If I hadn't run into your sister I wouldn't have known you were still alive."

"I'm sorry. I should have kept in touch. The work was

overwhelming, but that's no excuse. I thought about you. And I missed you." He looked deep into her eyes, so deeply she was afraid he could see the real reason she was leaving.

Isabel blinked back a tear. These were the words she longed to hear.

"I missed you too," she said softly.

"I shouldn't have gone. I should have sent someone else," he said, shaking his head. "I thought I was indispensable, the only one capable of doing the job, but when Guillermo came to relieve me I realized he was even better qualified than I was. He had the energy I had run out of. And Cosmo has taken over back here and done a great job. So maybe it was good I left as far as he was concerned. It's been a humbling experience to find I'm not as important as I thought. Except for one thing. You too decided you didn't need me."

"That's not true," she blurted. "The reason I'm leaving is that I need you too much." Now was the time to tell him how she felt. Then she could leave knowing she'd done her best and been honest with him. She'd have no regrets. She took a deep breath. " I...I...know we thought we were just having a good time, a summer fling, no strings, but somehow, even though I knew the rules, I couldn't help myself. I fell in love with you, Dario. Please don't say anything. I don't expect you to love me. I know how you feel. I know how much you've been hurt."

He reached across the table and took her hands in his. "I thought I'd never love again, you're right. I'd made such a colossal mistake, I lost all confidence in my judgment. I had myself convinced it was my destiny to be a loner, the black sheep in the family, the favorite uncle with no kids of his own. Then you came along and you changed my mind and you changed my life.

"I'll never forget that first day when you were determined to get to the Azienda in your ridiculous sandals and catch a ride back to town on a road that no one used. You just had to fix your own tires and grow your own grapes. I kept waiting for you to fail. But you always bounced back. I'd never met anyone like you. I didn't believe you could make it on your own."

"I can't," she said soberly.

"Yes, you can," he said and squeezed her hand. "But you don't have to. I want to be there for you whatever you want to do. I want to run the Azienda with you. I love you, Isabel. I want to marry you. I want to watch our children grow up together at the Azienda."

Isabel tilted her head to one side as if to see better, because her hearing must be affected. She thought she'd just heard Dario say he loved her.

After a long silence he spoke again. "Of course, if you don't feel the same…if you really want to get on that plane…" He stared at her as if willing her to tell him what he wanted to hear.

"No. No. I want to stay here with you. I came here to claim my inheritance and to find myself. A girl who'd never had a family or a home of her own. I wasn't sure I could manage by myself. Then you came along. You showed me how to scare off the wild boar, how to know when the grapes are ripe, how to change a tire and how to love again. You gave me the courage to do things I never thought I could. You introduced me to your family who I love as if they were my own. You challenged me and I hope you always will. I love you Dario. I loved you from the first moment I saw you picking grapes. I loved you even when you tried to talk me into buying another house. You wanted me to have an easier time."

"I confess, I wanted the Azienda. But I have something better. I have you. I should have known you'd choose the hard way. My stubborn Isabel. My darling Isabel." He brought her hands to his lips and kissed her fingers. "Don't cry," he said, with alarm as the tears gathered in her eyes. She'd tried so hard to be brave. She knew the penalty for crying. She'd learned early and learned well. But now the dam had burst she couldn't stop. She sobbed so loudly that other passengers turned and looked at her with sympathy.

Dario handed her his handkerchief. "Don't cry, Isabel. I love you. I can't promise you an easy life, but I can promise you a life that will never be boring." He stood and helped her out of her seat.

"Let's go home," he said, drawing her to him. "There are grapes to be picked, bells to ring and a wedding to plan." She threw her arms around him and kissed him as a flight to America was being announced on the loud speaker. It was a flight she would not be taking. Not today. Not without Dario.

EPILOGUE

On a sunny October day, the small stone church on the Villarmosa town square was full of friends and relatives for the wedding of Dario Montessori and his American bride, Isabel Morrison. No one who had ever seen them together in the weeks before their wedding could doubt they were meant for each other. They radiated happiness wherever they went, from the Azienda to his family home to the town of Agrigento where he bought her wedding ring and where they attended a performance of *The Marriage of Figaro*. The music made Isabel feel as romantic as any Sicilian in the audience. Everyone remarked that they made a perfect couple. Everyone seemed to have known they were meant for each other before the couple knew—especially the Montessori family.

He was rich, strong, tall and dazzlingly handsome in his black tuxedo and white shirt. She was beautiful, rich in spirit, and wore an ivory satin dress that set off her fiery auburn hair, the color of a Sicilian sunset.

They said their vows in English and Italian, then kissed while all the women watching dabbed the tears from their eyes and all the men smiled broadly. Dario Montessori had finally met his match. After the ceremony the bride showed off the results of her Italian lessons by engaging Dario's grandfather in conversation.

"*Sono cosi felice di fare parte della vostra famiglia,*" she said.

The old man beamed at her from his wheelchair.

Then it was off to the reception at the Azienda, now in the middle of reconstruction. Soon there would be a huge addition to the old house as well as a tasting room for visitors. Tables covered with white cloths and flowers were set up outside in the vineyard. A string quartet played Italian love songs. There were toasts in two languages. A temporary dance floor had been constructed with a view of the surrounding countryside.

After Dario toasted his bride, he took her aside and said, "Signora Montessori, I haven't given you your wedding present yet." He reached into his pocket and handed her a small black velvet box.

Inside was a small picture frame with a photo of a man with red hair. "Your uncle," he said. "I found the photo in the newspaper office. I'm sure if he knew what you've done to his vineyard, he would be proud of you. No one could deserve it more. No one could have done more for it than you. And there's no one I owe more to for bringing you to me."

"Thank you," she said, with a smile. "Now I know what he looked like. My only relative. I too thank him for bringing me here to Sicily and the Azienda."

He lifted his champagne glass. "To Uncle Antonio."

She tapped her glass against his.

"Your only relative until now. As of today you now have dozens." He gave a wide gesture toward the family members, all part of the wedding party from the flower girls and the ring bearers to the bridesmaids and groomsmen.

"I found an account of how he arrived a few years ago from America to make his way to Sicily," Dario said. He studied the tendrils of red-gold hair that framed her face. "I think I see a family resemblance."

"You mean the hair. I hope you're prepared for red-haired children."

"The more the better," he said, holding her so close she felt his heart beating in time with hers. "This will be a wonderful place for them to grow up. By the way, isn't it time to leave for our honeymoon?"

She looked around at the rows of vines, at the house with the new roof and the scaffolding and the framework for the addition. Her home. *Their* home. A wonderful place to live. A wonderful place for their children to grow up. A dream come true. When they returned from their honeymoon in Florence they'd move into his cottage until the remodeling was finished.

"I have a present for you too." She reached into the embroidered lace bodice of her gown and handed him a small gold key. "The key to my heart," she said.

He pressed the key to his lips, put it in his pocket and thanked whatever fates had sent him Isabel—his life and his love.

MILLS & BOON®
Pure reading pleasure™

MAY 2009 HARDBACK TITLES

ROMANCE

The Greek Tycoon's Blackmailed Mistress	Lynne Graham
Ruthless Billionaire, Forbidden Baby	Emma Darcy
Constantine's Defiant Mistress	Sharon Kendrick
The Sheikh's Love-Child	Kate Hewitt
The Boss's Inexperienced Secretary	Helen Brooks
Ruthlessly Bedded, Forcibly Wedded	Abby Green
The Desert King's Bejewelled Bride	Sabrina Philips
Bought: For His Convenience or Pleasure?	Maggie Cox
The Playboy of Pengarroth Hall	Susanne James
The Santorini Marriage Bargain	Margaret Mayo
The Brooding Frenchman's Proposal	Rebecca Winters
His L.A. Cinderella	Trish Wylie
Dating the Rebel Tycoon	Ally Blake
Her Baby Wish	Patricia Thayer
The Sicilian's Bride	Carol Grace
Always the Bridesmaid	Nina Harrington
The Valtieri Marriage Deal	Caroline Anderson
Surgeon Boss, Bachelor Dad	Lucy Clark

HISTORICAL

The Notorious Mr Hurst	Louise Allen
Runaway Lady	Claire Thornton
The Wicked Lord Rasenby	Marguerite Kaye

MEDICAL™

The Rebel and the Baby Doctor	Joanna Neil
The Country Doctor's Daughter	Gill Sanderson
The Greek Doctor's Proposal	Molly Evans
Single Father: Wife and Mother Wanted	Sharon Archer

0409 Gen Std LP

MILLS & BOON®
Pure reading pleasure™

MAY 2009 LARGE PRINT TITLES

ROMANCE

The Billionaire's Bride of Vengeance	Miranda Lee
The Santangeli Marriage	Sara Craven
The Spaniard's Virgin Housekeeper	Diana Hamilton
The Greek Tycoon's Reluctant Bride	Kate Hewitt
Nanny to the Billionaire's Son	Barbara McMahon
Cinderella and the Sheikh	Natasha Oakley
Promoted: Secretary to Bride!	Jennie Adams
The Black Sheep's Proposal	Patricia Thayer

HISTORICAL

The Captain's Forbidden Miss	Margaret McPhee
The Earl and the Hoyden	Mary Nichols
From Governess to Society Bride	Helen Dickson

MEDICAL™

Dr Devereux's Proposal	Margaret McDonagh
Children's Doctor, Meant-to-be Wife	Meredith Webber
Italian Doctor, Sleigh-Bell Bride	Sarah Morgan
Christmas at Willowmere	Abigail Gordon
Dr Romano's Christmas Baby	Amy Andrews
The Desert Surgeon's Secret Son	Olivia Gates

MILLS & BOON®

Pure reading pleasure™

JUNE 2009 HARDBACK TITLES

ROMANCE

The Sicilian's Baby Bargain	Penny Jordan
Mistress: Pregnant by the Spanish Billionaire	Kim Lawrence
Bound by the Marcolini Diamonds	Melanie Milburne
Blackmailed into the Greek Tycoon's Bed	Carol Marinelli
The Ruthless Greek's Virgin Princess	Trish Morey
Veretti's Dark Vengeance	Lucy Gordon
Spanish Magnate, Red-Hot Revenge	Lynn Raye Harris
Argentinian Playboy, Unexpected Love-Child	Chantelle Shaw
The Savakis Mistress	Annie West
Captive in the Millionaire's Castle	Lee Wilkinson
Cattle Baron: Nanny Needed	Margaret Way
Greek Boss, Dream Proposal	Barbara McMahon
Boardroom Baby Surprise	Jackie Braun
Bachelor Dad on Her Doorstep	Michelle Douglas
Hired: Cinderella Chef	Myrna Mackenzie
Miss Maple and the Playboy	Cara Colter
A Special Kind of Family	Marion Lennox
Hot Shot Surgeon, Cinderella Bride	Alison Roberts

HISTORICAL

The Rake's Wicked Proposal	Carole Mortimer
The Transformation of Miss Ashworth	Anne Ashley
Mistress Below Deck	Helen Dickson

MEDICAL™

Emergency: Wife Lost and Found	Carol Marinelli
A Summer Wedding at Willowmere	Abigail Gordon
The Playboy Doctor Claims His Bride	Janice Lynn
Miracle: Twin Babies	Fiona Lowe

0509 Gen Std LP

MILLS & BOON®

Pure reading pleasure™

JUNE 2009 LARGE PRINT TITLES

ROMANCE

The Ruthless Magnate's Virgin Mistress	Lynne Graham
The Greek's Forced Bride	Michelle Reid
The Sheikh's Rebellious Mistress	Sandra Marton
The Prince's Waitress Wife	Sarah Morgan
The Australian's Society Bride	Margaret Way
The Royal Marriage Arrangement	Rebecca Winters
Two Little Miracles	Caroline Anderson
Manhattan Boss, Diamond Proposal	Trish Wylie

HISTORICAL

Marrying the Mistress	Juliet Landon
To Deceive a Duke	Amanda McCabe
Knight of Grace	Sophia James

MEDICAL™

A Mummy for Christmas	Caroline Anderson
A Bride and Child Worth Waiting For	Marion Lennox
One Magical Christmas	Carol Marinelli
The GP's Meant-To-Be Bride	Jennifer Taylor
The Italian Surgeon's Christmas Miracle	Alison Roberts
Children's Doctor, Christmas Bride	Lucy Clark